THE MYSTERY OF LYSHAM MANOR

By

NanyWytch

To Micho e David lot of love Ashrer xxx

The mystery of Lysham Manor by NanyWytch

The mystery of Lysham Manor by NanyWytch

AUTHORS NOTE:

COPYRIGHT BELONGS TO NANYWYTCHWRITER.CO.UK

February 2021.

This genre is complete fiction; all characters are fictitious. Places used in the story are used to enhance a fictitious tale of the paranormal.

The moral right of the author has been asserted

All rights are reserved

Without limiting rights under copyright no part of this publication may be reproduced, stored or introduced into a retrieval system. Transmitted in any form or by any means electronic, mechanical or otherwise without the prior permission of the author and publisher of this book.

The mystery of Lysham Manor by NanyWytch

Dedicated to my father Mr James Ayrey

The mystery of Lysham Manor by NanyWytch

The mystery of Lysham Manor by NanyWytch

The mystery of Lysham Manor by NanyWytch

PREFACE

Lysham Manor is the largest sprawling estate in Haworth West riding Yorkshire. Not only is it a fine house with a wonderful garden, tended by its own gardener Symons. It boasts a farming community. Houses its own workers, not only on the farm but in house. It is the only upper-class house in the area, which has stood over 500 years in one family the proud family Gaunt.

This is the story of this house, what dwells within its walls. House's soak up energies created by families over time, this house is bleeding ghosts. However, things are never as they seem, life can throw in unexpected events, as well as few surprises. A young 18-year-old girl has travelled from Devon to Haworth over 8 days, walking during the day staying in taverns at night. To see her only living relative her aunt Jessica. However, before she arrives her aunt dies, she is buried next to her husband Henry in Haworth cemetery. With only 9 pennies to her name in 1857, she wanders the road in an awfully bad storm, with just a wool cloak for warmth. She finds an old house along the road near the moors, desperate cold and wet she knocks on the door.

The mystery of Lysham Manor by NanyWytch

Summary of characters

Sir Fredrick John Gaunt an elderly gentleman, well-liked by the villagers and servants 6'4 tall grey hair blue eyes

John Gaunt eldest son, selfish gambling drunk; aged 21, 6'2 tall red curly hair red beard red moustache neatly trimmed, green eyes. Well educated at Eton harsh to staff and bully

Daniel Gaunt youngest son weak willed, easily manipulated by his big brother; exceptionally good artist he painted Eileen opened a gallery, became well known and wealthy. 5'6 tall blonde hair blue eyes clean-shaven well-mannered gentleman educated at Eton

Aunt Jessica lives in a country house in Mytholmroyd near the mill

Elizabeth Angeles wife to Sir Fredrick died 16th May year of our Lord 1845, beautiful lady died in childbirth to a daughter who died with her

Francis's James Baines's lawyer & son Jonathan Francis Baines, junior partner highly trained lawyers only law firm in Haworth village

Sarah Hunt; the Cook worked in the manor for 20 years, until dismissed by Master John to care for his bastard child her main love was cooking

Symonds; much loved gardener Fredrick's best friend from childhood, as his father was the head gardener on the estate. 6'1 tall wear a trilby hat, brown baggy trousers, have reddish brown hair rough beard aged 62

The mystery of Lysham Manor by NanyWytch

Marshal Roche; stable boy loved horses; he was also the odd job man. He is a muscular guy clean shaven wears open collarless shirt, loose trousers riding boots brown hair

Dr Stroud the family's doctor & his son Dr Paul Stroud, are stout men one is 5'5" the other 5'7" tended family since boys born

Reverend William Annand the village preacher, tall dark hair rather stout, dresses in black he's 5'9 tall has a tidy tach and very groomed beard he has known family since Fredrick's marriage to his wife

John Benson contriver by trade, marries Eleanor Hunt, he is tall at 6'3 muscular man business orientated loves his young vibrant wife. Well educated well liked for his designs.

Eleanor Hunt illegitimate daughter of John Gaunt she is a tiny woman of 5'3 very thin but bouncy well known in village loves dances and reads a lot.

Eileen Mason Perry, becomes the companion to Sir Fredrick extremely ambitious, young lady who got lost in a storm. Inherits the manor much to the anger of John she is just 18 when she arrives penniless.

Leah upper house maid, worked at house till Daniel dies came at 14, is skinny yet rather lovely girl adores Daniel tolerates johns' moods.

Mary lower house maid works till Daniel dies she is a stout girl short at 5'3 dark haired pretty thing miserable most of time

The mystery of Lysham Manor by NanyWytch

George the gamekeeper, resides in the house in the woods he hunts rabbits' birds keep the woods balanced his wife works at the house as under housemaid.

Sarah scullery maid, daughter to the Cook she is 14 wants go work at the mill as its more money her mother will not allow it. She is a silly girl always trying avoid working

Edward's footman, nephew of Henry he is stout man of around 20 quite responsible only male servant to upstairs helps dress the men.

Joe's boy from farm not much known but has red hair curly

Farm labour's

Farm labour's wives and children dwell in the tide cottages on the land they can plant food and keep goats & chickens

The mystery of Lysham Manor by NanyWytch

Chapter one

John Benson stands amidst the burnt-out ruins of his house Lysham Manor. John a civic engineer by trade was here to design, and build the new hospital. He is very well known in London. His talents in design and engineering wanted by many to design or indeed expand an existing premise's. He held many citations that praised his worth.

A few months prior 18 months to be exact he had married the love of his life young vibrant beautiful angelic Eleanor, after dating her over 3 years.

The couple met at the village barn dance, held at the old school rooms. They moved into the manor just 18 months ago. Now his wife was dead!

The manor had laid empty sadly neglected for the past 14 years standing within its own rather overgrown grounds. Over just a few months, John had totally refurbished the house, gardens and the farm. He was just starting on. Demolishing the North wing, to use the Yorkshire stone to rebuild the stables and farm housing. John and his surveyor had looked around the house with a view to buying it, they wrote down a list with costs. Whilst there they both felt something following them. Each time they turned nothing was there. On the way out a woman walked down the stairs as if not aware of them into the library. John was in a buying mood went to see the lawyers who told him an heir had been found.

Back home his wife had been given a pack of legal papers stating she was now the owner of this manor and lands

The mystery of Lysham Manor by NanyWytch

Not long after they moved into the huge desolate place

Initially his wife was fine. A few weeks into being on site Eleanor started to hear voices nobody else heard she swore they were coming out the walls and mirrors. she heard voices often calling her up to the top rooms. Dr Stroud diagnosed nervous depression; he knew the family history, but he was keeping very tight lipped.

On his many visits his son Paul would accompany him on the latest visit he could get no further than the bedroom door. Dr Stroud returns to the library to John saying.

'I am sorry sir; but if your wife will not allow me into the room, there is little to nothing I can do to help. You must remove her from here Sir, I feel this dark place might be making things far worse. Maybe taking her away on that honeymoon you talked about, somewhere warm less secluded. I will call again if you wish on the morrow.'

'Yes, yes please feel free to call as much as you feel necessary. I trust you will send over the bill for your services Sir. '

'Of course, I can drop it off with you tomorrow, might I say you have done some fine work in such a short time, on the manor. It is starting to resemble its past now. It was the most imposing place in the whole area, I do have an incredibly old sketch of the place drawn by my father, if you might care to see it. It has the whole front of the east wing. You do know that this place has an odd building in the midst of the woods. I believe the game keeper lived there. '

'Of course, that would be lovely maybe you would care to stay to dinner, you can tell me about this place. I love to learn about old places but here I know nothing at all.'

'I do not mind if I do, I had no other calls to make today, it would be nice to reminisce.'

Dr Stroud puts down his bag and coats settle in a chair near the fire, John offers him a drink, 'brandy, port wine or whiskey Sir? which is to your taste?''

'A brandy will be nice its rather cold out there today.'

'Have you seen your wife today Sir?' asks the Dr

'No, she refused allow me into the room, so I slept elsewhere' John replies

"Strange this! she is such a pretty little thing, it is odd that her behaviours are altered so much, in the village she was favoured by everyone for her manners, the fact she would help anyone at all no matter what class they were. It worries me it really does."

'Tell me about the place? I mean by this more about its design and history.'

'It has been in the family I think over 500 years now, it was built by Sir Fredrick's grandfather back in the late 1700s. I believe there ought to be a painting of him, on the walls in long gallery upstairs.

Obviously, it could have been moved. My history with the family began when the boys were born to Fredrick and Elizabeth, she died giving birth to a daughter who died with

The mystery of Lysham Manor by NanyWytch

her in 1845 complications arose during the birth. We lost them both sadly. It almost destroyed Fredrick; his boys were sent away to school; you see the house was so incredibly quiet without them.'

'Have you ever spent the night here? Asks John

'Oh yes on many occasions Elizabeth loved to hold dances and parties. She was such a gracious hostess. I do believe I slept in one of the rooms in the west wing, it was a splendid room, the decor impressed me the most every room so different. Elizabeth chose all the decor and furnishings herself. She had a good eye.' Dr Stroud says to John

John then tells Dr Stroud how he finds the place quite creepy

all those narrow dark, passages with the empty rooms, The Dr says' yes I do suppose you might, you see when Elizabeth was alive. She had around 35 servants here. The house was always busy, the boys noticeably younger they had several nannies for some reason; they did not stay long complained of strange things going on in the nursery.'

'Yes, John says it is a rather large house. There are parts of this house, I have never stepped.'

'In time John as you have redone the interior maybe you will hold the winter ball. It is something to aim for'.

Yes, indeed my wife would love that, maybe it would very much bring her back to me Dr replies John he continues

'The darkness that pervades some areas has the back of my neck tingle'

'Yes, I didn't go to many rooms here myself. So, I would be none the wiser Sir. '

They continue their conversation over another brandy.

'We have employed 26 staff, but Leah is the one servant, who has worked here since she was just 14 years old, now she is the one in charge of the staff. Have you met her such a nice young lady.?'

'Not really Sir I might have seen her about years ago, but the place lay empty desolate for the past 14 years after Daniel died. Nobody knew if there was an heir to be had. '

Eleanor walked in; Dr Stroud was shocked at her appearance, she looked years older, her face drawn pale, her eyes had dark circles around them, she was very jumpy nervous. Her hair once kept so nicely fastened up, enhanced her features but today it was unkempt tangled dragged down her back.

Her eyes bore a haunted expression of someone very afraid. In fact, they were full of fear, she sat down on a chair looking at her husband.

'I am sorry, Eleanor says 'I could not allow you into my room you see its rather a mess, I have not slept, I cannot the voices they call to me at night. I try to shut them out really, I do but they frighten me. The shadows that come into my room taunt me; I know you think I am over wrought; but really Dr something is so terribly wrong here. I wish we had stayed in the village in our small, tiny cottage'.

'John maybe we could,

The mystery of Lysham Manor by NanyWytch

John replies 'I am sorry darling but we sold the cottage do not you remember.

Eleanor stumbles over the words 'Oh yes, I well, no not really, I know we talked about this,''

'Yes, darling it sold almost as soon as the sign went up. We could go away on our belated honeymoon, but it can now only be for a month.'

Eleanor says 'Maybe we move to the other cottage we inherited'.

'Darling we rented it out do not you remember, what Mr Blaine said about investing.'

'Yes, John maybe we ought to go away your right, can I think about it. Choose a place,

John answers his wife 'Of course, my love.

She asks 'Is Dr Stroud staying for dinner? we must tell Leah, 'Of course we had not long sat down, we were talking about the house. Says John to her

Eleanor sounds frightened 'Oh, no I would rather not discuss that maybe, I will leave you go tell the staff we have a guest for dinner. Its lamb today is that alright you do eat meat? Dr Stroud 'yes anything as a man living alone, I enjoy the company of others when I get invited it breaks up my days. Otherwise, it's all patients and hospital no pleasure.'

'Excuse me gentlemen I will join you for dinner, I need to ask one of the maids to tend me'. Eleanor leaves the two men in the lounge. She goes to the kitchen to inform her staff about the extra person dining tonight, then asks for one of the girls to assist her in dressing for dinner. Eleanor and Mary go upstairs to the room. Where, she chooses her red gown. Mary takes out the other items needed then starts to brush her mistress's hair they chat to each other

'Eleanor asks Mary if she finds upstairs rather strange in some areas especially the east wing."

"Mary tells her it creeps her out being alone in that wing. That the rest of the place doesn't have that chill, with the feeling of being watched."

"I agree says Eleanor have you ever seen these shadows come from mirrors like people who talk to you?"

"No miss why?"

"I hear these voices at night and I see this man and a woman mostly but she is terrifying she has these long nails all twisted. Her face is contorted like she was screaming it's so awful. At first I thought I was dreaming, but Mary I don't think I am. "

"Your wife; she looks fearful and rather exhausted might I suggest I prescribe something to help her sleep. How long has she spoken about voices?" mentions the Dr

John says "Oh those a few days is all, she was wandering around in the night, in the dark swearing someone was here. But we searched the place to find nobody about. She does worry me. She claims these shadows come out of the mirrors in our room she has removed the mirrors. She has changed so much since we have been here, maybe I ought to get her a

The mystery of Lysham Manor by NanyWytch

companion another lady someone she can spend time with? I am away a lot during the day working."

The Dr says "Yes, it would help spending so much time alone is not good for someone. What happened to Mercy and Julie her friends, from Haworth and Cornfield.?"

"Well, the truth is we haven't spent any time alone here as a couple, because of the work being done. So, I am afraid I am guilty of asking them to leave" John replies

"I see well maybe rethink it, but do take her away somewhere a month will be great. Says the Dr

'Might I ask how you inherited the manor.?" asks Dr Stroud

John replies "Well, it was rather odd actually come to think on it now. We had a letter from a lawyer, a Mr Francis Baines he said he had traced Eleanor as being the illegitimate daughter of Johnathon Paul Gaunt. Obviously had there been a legitimate heir, they would have inherited but apparently, she was the only one, so it came to her. We were told her mama was a woman called Eileen Mason Perry. We inherited the art gallery plus two cottages in Haworth. It was a huge shock to Eleanor as she thought Sarah was her mother.

Sarah brought her up from being a baby, but she was not adopted. Do you see how odd this sounds; I really need to know more as I need to help my wife? You see I married Eleanor Hunt not Gaunt so do we actually have a legal claim. Is my wife a Hunt at all? Will it make our wedding certificate invalid if she is a Gaunt.?"

The mystery of Lysham Manor by NanyWytch

"It does sound a bit odd; I never knew John had any children at all, Daniel never mentioned a niece to me, which brings about another question do you have any pictures of this woman said to be her mother?" mentions the Dr

"No, the lawyer only had very scarce details. "Replies John

A servant knocks and enters

"Gentlemen dinner will be served in the dining room"

"Thank you, Edward Is my wife down yet? No Sir, do you want the maid to check she is joining us as she mentioned earlier. Yes, tell her to come to us."

"Of course, Sir"

"Shall we go to the dining room we dine at 7pm promptly in an evening says John

They walk towards the dining room and sit down

"Excuse me, Sir, says Edward your wife is not upstairs, the maid says she was dressed over an hour ago, to join you here. "

"Where on earth can she have gone in her evening gown? Is her wrap missing?"

"No Sir she is not wearing her shoes either, Mary laid them out for her."

"We had best inform Leah keep the food warm get the male staff to go search outside, we will cover inside"

The mystery of Lysham Manor by NanyWytch

"of course, Sir "says Edward will you wish to speak to Mary Sir she was with your wife last.'

'Yes, Edward have her sent up she might give us a clue.'

Mary arrives' you sent for me Sir'

'Indeed, Mary I did, when you attended the mistress how did she seem to you?'

'Well Sir replies Mary to the Master of the house, she was very calm and quite happy at having the Dr stay to dinner.

As I brushed her hair before we pinned it up. She spoke about these dark. Shadows coming from the mirrors, as soon as we had completed her hair, she covered the mirror with a silk shawl.'

"So, when you left the mistress where was she?"

'Sat on her window seat muttering to herself about voices. Will that be all Sir?'

"Yes, Mary thank you we will talk later "

'Yes Sir'

They all begin searching for Eleanor, she is on the top floor trying to find where the voices are coming from. She enters a room with a window seat, it smells of decay. Cobwebs drift attached to things they look like tiny tendrils ready to capture the prey. Inside one Web sits a rather large spider, who is waiting for his dinner to walk to him. She watches the hunter and prey dance the death rites. The voices are here they are coming from the covered mirror. She drags it off the mirror.

The mystery of Lysham Manor by NanyWytch

She looks behind it. She shivers realising she has no shawl it's very cold she can see her breathe. The voices start to talk again whispering into her head.

Eleanor come we are looking for you, Eleanor listens to the song. She hums the tune, recalls this but where from has no idea. Look Eleanor look.

The mirror on the dresser has Words on it, rallec, rallec, emoc, listen to us we will help you stay with us. After all you belong with us. Tnuag. Eleanor leaves her room to climb up to the unused part of the house the old east wing.led by these unseen shadows and voices.

Eleanor sits in the attic room in the much-forgotten East Wing, it smells damp, its cold, colder than it ought to be for this time of year. Dust hangs about like a carpet covering everything around her. Looking in the mirror at her much-altered features, she hates what she sees. Then she sees another woman in the mirror; and hears these words run away child as I never wanted a baby ever, you just a product of rape, is what you are unwanted Hated, you must die, so I may be free.

picking up the chair Eleanor hurls it into the mirror shattering it into small, jagged pieces. That voice taunts her constantly. She shouts leave me the hell alone whoever you are. Eleanor thinks she is losing her sanity. John the love of her life cannot hear these voices nor can he see these people inside mirrors around the place. The Dr says he cannot see them either, nor Leah.

The mystery of Lysham Manor by NanyWytch

She dreaded the nights for the voice she could hear hammering into her brain, the one thing she wanted above all else was sleep. John was in utter desperation, he could not hear these voices, nor see these shadows, his lady spoke about. So, he assumed they were delusions he was worried that she might harm herself. He realised that this illness began within 18 months of residing in this grim place called Lysham Manor. With its sprawling gardens and woodland. When he met her, through the years before they married, she was an extremely healthy 26-year-old girl with more life in her always smiling and dancing she loved the dances. Now she was 29 approaching her 30th birthday

The following day when Dr Stroud called, John was insistent, they must get into Eleanor room, he had last seen her with cuts the night before when they found her crying in the attic amongst the broken glass. As they walked up the stairs which wound around to the hall, above a huge crash was heard, so John burst down the door to his wife's room. She was again covered in glass as she had again broken a mirror claiming a man was after her saying he would kill her.

"My darling there is no man in your room, but he's over there can you not see him leering at me with those dark eyes, the red hair like a mass of curls. John I am so very frightened help me"

"Dr Stroud said I think I need give her a sedative; she has not slept in days overtiredness can give a person hallucination. Yes, rest and sleep are what she needs."

"Seriously Dr I need to know what is happening here. She claims these shadows step right out of mirrors."

"I will join you in a moment after making sure your wife is sleeping. I may have an inkling as to what is wrong."

John sends the maid to clean up the glass. Mary hates this part of the house, especially the round tower room this was her room, that weird girl turned up here filthy dirty. Who said she could be a witch, promised sew my mouth! shut for making up stories in the kitchens? I would not have let her into my home. Something wasn't right about her. Get out of my room girl, the ghost says standing inside the mirror. Mary jumps seeing the spirit right there in walks out of the mirror she is cleaning the glass quickly cold runs down her back. Mary runs away as quickly as she could. Arrives down the back stairs, frozen saying someone was there. I saw someone in the room.

 Leah laughs at her; don't be stupid girl the lady is sleeping and the master is in the library with his guest. He wanted the old chest bringing from the old master's room.

Mary was claiming that room creeps me out really bad. It is always so cold up there now,"

"Yeah, says Leah it has not had a fire since she vanished. Plus, it is December"

"Do not laugh its creepy this place sometimes, if your alone in parts of it."

"Awe do you want me send Edward with you next time, you are cleaning" laughs Leah laughing at Mary. Mary screams at Leah "stop it I was being serious."

The mystery of Lysham Manor by NanyWytch

"Hey, says Sarah I will not have squabbling in my kitchen now let us have our tea".

Dr Stroud joins John in the library, this room has floor to ceiling bookshelves made from mahogany, a sliding ladder to get to the higher shelves. It has the two-winged back leather chairs you can hide inside. Plus, the long narrow table in the middle. where John is currently searching an old chest for information about the house. He finds an old design of the house in a file. It looks vastly different from today in fact a whole wing is missing. Plus, in the cellar it looks like there are three rooms. We only found the one large room. Look here the attic in the east wing where are these rooms here. He points to the plan showing around eight servants' rooms. Awe this is an incredibly old drawing Fredrick's, father James Gaunt modernised the manor, maybe he made the cellar into the one room. Those rooms were burnt down in a fire, not sure they even exist now. They were just servants' rooms for when larger parties brought their own with them.

The Dr begins after pouring himself a brandy on John's invitation to stay to dinner again, it is quite a long story, but I might have some notion as to what is causing the problem.

I looked through my father's old papers he mentions that the North Wing was burnt down some years ago. There has been a lot of strange things occur in this place since, that fire. Many lives were lost some servants died along with Sir Fredrick's sister.

"Delusions it seems were quite common in some family members. For example, Fredrick's mother lived here for some time she claimed people followed her about the house strange see-through figures. The sister claimed she saw shadows in the older parts of the house. That these vanished through the mirrors, she had them all removed to the attic. "

"Maybe a genetic trait. In the past a few members were sent to the York asylum. You do know Daniel died there! No, I had no idea did he hear voices and see shadows lurking in mirrors.? Not sure but we ought to find out. "

"Do you want to go tomorrow? I can move my appointments to the afternoon, as a Dr I can gain access to areas you would not be permitted? We need to see the room and his files. Plus speak to the staff about him and a diagnosis. York Asylum is a huge nasty place, a warning I must give you before you step inside."

"Yes, we simply need to know if Daniel claimed the same as my Eleanor about the mirrors."

They sat near the blazing fire drinking brandy as the Dr Stroud told John the story of the manor to his knowledge .

The mystery of Lysham Manor by NanyWytch

Chapter two

Appearance

The storm raged the rain fair danced on the road, making visibility hard. Yet that smell of freshness of the air that comes with a storm was lovely. Eileen Mason Perry a pretty young girl of 18 years was arriving in the small village of Haworth. To stay with her widowed aunt Jess. Only to find her aunt had died the week before, was now buried in the cemetery next to her late husband, the house was all locked up. With what little money she had she had been unsure if it would even cover one night at the tavern. Down south the rooms with food and washing had cost around 12d. She pulls her thin wool, wet cloak around her tightly her feet so wet they squelched as she walked, her fingers frozen from the chill of the night's dampness.

What if it was not enough for a meal to warm her, she had slept in some very nasty places that cost 6d a night 2d for stew and bread 1d for cheapest ale having only nine pennies left to her name. She decided to just walk up the hill towards the church, the cobbled Street was very dark having the open sewer gulley run down one side. main street. Water gushed down over the cobbles filling this gulley dragging its contents down the main part of the path. Part way up she stopped to rest as the hill became steeper right near the midden the stench was awful. The midden was full to bursting of rotting animal waste, placed there by the butchers 6 of them on this one stretch. Just near where she stood, she could see four outhouses, overflowing into the street due to the rain it was a common occurrence before main street had sewers. A man stood smoking on his doorstep, evening he nodded.

"Are you lost?"

"No Sir the hill is steep,"

"Aye you gets used to it, you are not from these parts are you lass".

"No Sir from Devon that is an awfully long way are you here on holiday? "

"No Sir my aunt died she is now buried in the church at the top am going there in the morning". Why don't you come inside out of the rain lass we can dry you by the fire give you some soup and tea"

"Thank you, Sir that would be very welcome." He shouts to his wife

"Hey Heather I just been called Sir first time in my life love."

"I do hope I have not offended Sir". Says Eileen

"No lass you have not, you have cheered up an old man". Eileen went inside met Heather and Bob who lived on Lodge Street. The cottage was small but quaint and so warm. The fireplace dominated this room, it was also where they cooked. The rest would refresh her she thought her legs ached. It would be nice to remove these wet things actually feel warm again. She sat with them near the fire they ate broth and chunks of fresh bread. Drank copious amounts of hot tea. Bob said "why don't you stay here tonight continue in the morning lass we have room."

"I don't want to impose on you sir",

"My dear girl you are not imposing you can talk to us dear losing your aunt must be a shock" after travelling so far how many miles away from here is it to your village?"

"Yes, indeed it is I have travelled from Devon my village is Cloverlly it situated on one very steep hill with a cobbled road like this village, it has a marina down at the bottom where the sea is often very rough. It's a fishing village. Yes, Sir its 323 miles exactly."

"So, did you travel by train lass? All alone as well you are brave."

"Some of the way yes, I took 3 trains but the last 70 miles I walked as money was getting tight having stayed in taverns at night."

"You poor Lass let me look at your boots love, I am a cobbler by trade I can fix them up for you." "Why thank you they leak now my feet are wet" I was thinking they have huge holes in them now.

"Heather says come on sweet child let's get you into something dry and warm."

They go up the stone curved steps that are well worn on the edges. Heather finds her a warm nightdress and warm dry socks, then gives her a wool shawl as well now lass we will dry your clothes shall we they will be good as new in the morning.

You know its ok to cry if your upset love we won't mind. Who was your aunt lass"? Her name was Jess Hunt

"She lived on Mytholmroyd Road near the mill there. I knew Jess lass, we worked together in the weaving shed. Till she took sick a few months ago the master let her go he got a new younger version.

"Did you go her funeral?

"Yes, we did it was only 3 days ago lass. Pity you missed it. The lawyer will have locked up the place, he knew someone was coming called Eileen Mason Perry, yes but do please call me Elle"

"Oh, lass your aunt was so poorly we took her calf foot jelly, and some Coltsfoot medicine for her cough. She kept asking for her elly, DR said her chest gave out. Her lungs love they just couldn't cope against the infection you see love it is the fluff off the looms you breathe it in and Jess worked over 10 years in weaving shed to my knowledge. It's very nice to have your company lass. We have an early start in the morning let's hope tomorrow is better for you. The lawyer is near top of hill love not far from cemetery. Come on lass let it out just sob your little heart out will make you feel better. I will give you some flowers from the garden put on her grave. Remind me in the morning. Now let's just sit here and recall funny things about your aunt, I am sure we have seen you afore when you were small. Yes,"

"I has been here before on holidays" They chatted about her aunts' silly sense of humour the jokes she told it was nice hear what someone else knew of her aunt. At around 9pm they went to bed; she had the back room with a double bed in it with cream wool blankets and the flock mattress. The bed was so cosy she slept very well indeed.

The next morning it was dry but damp the sky looked very black like thunder was coming, it felt so heavy, she walked up the hill, with Heather to the graveyard. They placed flowers at the grave then Heather left her alone there. Pop in for a brew later love. The lawyer will have left keys at the manor up on top near moors lass. I believe her cottage was owned by those at the manor. Thank you for last night you rescued me. "Aye love I would rescue you anytime. "

Elle sat on her aunts grave the tears came again, she was trying think what to do, after weeping so much she did feel a little lighter in herself. But she was going call on the lawyer's office see if he was there speak to. She wandered back down to the lawyer's office; he was not expected back for three days she was told but he has the keys. "I cannot release them until you have signed the papers lass am sorry have a good day the assistant said opening the door for her."

"Sir without those keys I have no place to go "

"You could try the manor they will have a set being as they own the place."

"I am so sorry miss but it is the law, I am only the assistant so sorry I cannot allow you the set here, but do try the manor it's about 3 mile walk all up hill." She left feeling things just were not going her way.

A woman was shouting at her husband calling him a drunken fool. Eileen carried on seeing the Black Bull tavern with its large stables and turning point. Men standing outside smoking and drinking, laughing about their day. She went inside to see how much it would be for two nights board. Timothy the landlord said its 6d a night here lass. Thank you, Sir. She had a drink of juice and left. This meant she had only eight pennies to her name meaning one night there possibly however she thought she may need the money if she got the keys at this house. she might need this for food she felt as if she were destitute. She sat on the church steps, trying to think about what to do next. The rain started again the street emptied quickly. She took herself into the church at least it was dry. She spoke to the priest, about her aunt and uncle's grave. About her issues of not getting into the house. He said then you need pray to God that he grants thee help lass. "There is work going at the mills Ivy bank lane I heard yesterday they were looking for people with nimble fingers"

"Thank you, Sir that is a help."

She walked down to the mill at ivy Lane, the Overseer took her the office. The mill Master said I am sorry lass the vacancies have all been filled. Thank you, Sir, she said. Leaving the mill.

She looked in some shops enquired how much a train ticket home would cost her. £3 she did not have. As her day went on the weather turned worse come 5pm when most people were about to have tea, she walked up the hill again.

The mystery of Lysham Manor by NanyWytch

The water pump being just outside the Black Bull she managed get a drink of water. Opposite was a place named ganger's croft was the poorest housing in the village with 24 families crowded into basement accommodation. she could not afford the fare of a Hackney carriage takes her back home. So, she decided go find this manor she walked along the country road in this raging sleet getting colder by the second. No idea what to do, she was about to turn around go back towards Black Bull tavern freezing & drenched now, shivering. The thunder started crashing through the sky lightening came minutes after, the rain was coming down now in buckets.

Having walked 4¼ of a mile, she saw a large gate with the name Lysham Manor emblazoned into the wrought iron gates with the blacksmiths sigils, she knew meant the name Hogg a particularly good Smith. She thought maybe she could ask for work; she was no stranger to hard work. When her parents died, she was sent the workhouse. She then worked in a mill for over 8 years of her life. Singletons mill owner found it cheaper to have children from aged 8 years to 18 live in the mill boarding houses, feed them twice per day. Give them just ½ days schooling per week, as indentured labour. Simply because he did not need to pay them. They worked for food and lodging which was not great for the young ones. 12 hour shifts near on killed many. When they got too sick to work, he sent them back to the workhouse claimed a replacement. So, there was always a need to find more. back home often these big estates needed staff. Workhouse sold them on at only five pounds per person. Having lost workers from the farms, to the growing mills this village had several already pumping out that black smoke. She pushed open the gates which creaked loudly as wind dragged the trees to near bent in half.

The rain incessantly beating down, thunder crashed across the sky lighting up the twisted drive, as she walked each time the lightening crashed, she jumped out of the way a nearby tree crashes to the ground.

She walked steadily wrapping her cloak more tightly about her even though it now lacked any warmth. An owl hoots from a nearby tree causing her to jump in fright. She stares straight at it as it looks back at her, before flying off then diving down almost in front of her, rising up with a mouse held firm in its claws. At least it has got dinner. Her stomach growls, a bowl of porridge Heather had made her this morning was all she had eaten. She has reached the large double fronted doorway, ivy clings around the posts supporting the overhang of the porch, it creeps up the walls like some alien creature using its teeth to grip the ancient stones. The Manor was this huge imposing house with lots of windows and curved corners, it was built in Yorkshire stone. The attics tiny windows sat back looked dark and foreboding, but she knocks on the door using the strange knocker shaped like roman soldier. The round Tower at each end looked like good-sized rooms, its tall chimneys with thick smoke leaking out. After what seemed an eternity to her a servant girl answered the door. She looked at Eileen's bedraggled appearance and in extremely poor English said

"What you be wanting at this time of night, if you be a gypsy be on your way afore I set the dogs after thee."

"Please miss is the master of the house in tonight. "She heard a man's voice

"Who is its Mary are they lost! "

I do not know who she be Sir, she is wet through looks half dead from cold shall I let her in Sir?"

A tall elderly gentleman came to the door. Eileen explained about her aunt said she wanted to know if he might have somewhere, she might sleep tonight, or if he needed any maids, she swore she would sleep in the kitchens if he would just allow her somewhere warm to rest.

"My dear child you can come in you look exhausted and soaked to the skin. To get such news as you arrive must be such a shock. I will have Leah find you something to wear, you may rest here tonight I would not wish even my dogs outside in this inclement weather"

Three hounds came charging down the stairs running right past her, after sniffing her. Pushing the slight wet girl about with wet noses, bed said the man the dogs strolled off towards the library.

She entered the huge hallway with it elegant, tiled floor in reds, yellows and blue embossed style. with just one exceptionally large Turkish rug near the stairs which twisted around towards the top. Eileen had never seen a hallway as large as this one. Paintings hung along the length of the stairs a crystal candelabra, lit up the hallway casting its light over its splendour. Leaving the crevices dark and foreboding she had this creepy feeling crawl over her body as if being watched, a place this size would need quite a few staff.

Eileen was dripping all over the floor, she kept apologising for making a mess, the gentleman addressed his servant

"Mary be good enough take this young lady to my wife's old rooms find her something dry to wear from the linen closet up there."

"Of course, Sir is she to sleep there Yes, do so then once in dry clothing bring her into the drawing room. Sir maybe she can stay in the east wing the room at the corner tower was cleaned earlier Sir."

Mary said to the girl as the master wanders back into the room on the left of the hall, closely followed by these huge Irish wolf hounds. Whom had come strolling back to their master?

"Come on then best take them wet boots off here, don't want you coating these stairs in mud. I am the one who has cleaned them. "

Elle slipped off her wet boots and the wool socks she had worn. The socks dripped more water into the puddle she now stood in. Her feet were so very cold they were blue. She follows Mary up the main stairs, then along an awfully long corridor these halls were lined in portraits and odd pieces of furniture like they had been abandoned there. Along another corridor into a sparsely furnished room with plain cream walls. But a highly decorated ceiling the walls in here had a hint of pink plaster peeled off the walls it smelt of decay. One large metal bed frames a pillow and blankets plus a chair. The mattress was rolled up and tied with rope. One candle sat in a small holder it did not cast much light at all.

Mary announced she would be back in a minute with clothes Eileen said "is this my room? "

"Heavens no miss these rooms are not used much master would sack me if I even thought of selecting these rooms." Eileen shivered removing her wet things one layer at a time. Everything was wringing wet. "

"Then why bring me here? "

"Well, I mean you cannot have the mistress's room, it is far too grand for the likes of you that be the plain truth of it miss whoever you are. "

The maid returned with under garments, petticoat, corset and a dress of black linen remarkably simple clothes much like she was wearing, plus a pair of black wool socks that came up over the knees. She hands Eileen a towel to dry her long-bedraggled hair. Helping her to dress she says "

"Reckon Master be soft allowing uninvited females into his house of a night folks he dun no from Adam that is."

It felt good have dry things on especially the warm socks.

"I am sorry you feel that way maybe we will be working together soon if your Master needs more staff, so if I were you, I would be quiet."

"Be like that then your rude ungrateful wench. When ready go downstairs the way, we came and do not touch anything the master dun no like being kept waiting. "

The mystery of Lysham Manor by NanyWytch

"Are you just abandoning me?

"Yeah of course I am you are not that nice, why should I wait here when my food is going cold in the kitchen. I will send Leah up here, so you do not go wandering about. "

Off stomps Mary to get her dinner.

Eileen dresses quickly she is not sure what to do about her own clothing so leaves them on the floor for now. Thinking she had no idea how to get back downstairs.

"Leah comes in says hello are you ready meet the master now. "

"Yes of course why was Mary so abrupt with me? "

"She is hungry she gets right grumpy when she is hungry", says Leah

"Do not we all when thinking about food. Says Elle

"I would not mind her come along miss."

"Oh, do not call me miss its Eileen but I prefers Elle for short, so why bring me up to this floor if the rooms are no longer used."

"Awe well Mary does not much care for strangers miss, she thinks you be a gypsy or a witch even."

Eileen says maybe "I am a witch, who will cast a spell on her for making up stories about me in the kitchens."

"Miss Elle stop making me laugh, you would get know Mary is a nervous sort. what type of spell might it be? "A anti gossip spell, where we sew mouths shut." She giggles at Leah. They got along really well

Leah escorts her to the drawing room, this room was bright the fireplace was made from wood-stained lighter with the family crest in the middle section. All the walls were panelled in the same wood, the large Turkish rug in faded red meets the slate hearth with the padded fender guard you could sit on around the fire. Two really large fabric winged back chairs dominated by this beautiful hearth that shone in the candlelight. She waits for the master say if he requires anything more,

"Leah, can you ask the Cook send up some warm broth with bread and butter we will have a pot of tea and ask cook if she might send some of her nice lemon drizzle cake, please "

"of course, Sir. "

"Come on now lass sit by the fire warm thee self-up where has thee come from? "

Eileen is fascinated with this room she glances about at the furnishings in here but obeys the kind gentleman sits near the fire. She roasts her feet as near as she dares get to the fender surrounding the fire it had a cushioned top you could sit with you back to the fire. Slowly she stops shivering. Eileen's eyes wander about the room it could be a library the walls are literally full of books. In piles on the floor and this really nice large sideboard embossed with lions. Eileen absolutely loved books the furnishings are of the best oak, quite elaborate for such a room there was quiet an impressive desk here too maybe it was a study instead. She saw the pre-addressed stationary saying Elizabeth Gaunt the glass ink bottles and sand container, the quills all skilfully placed. The room just beyond the place looked far more homely, she could see it through its open door the old man said "

"Come on young lady we will go across the hall into the room you are gazing at. I must agree it is my favourite room in the whole place, Leah will bring our tea here. "

The smell of fresh cut flowers, met her nose as they entered, a beautiful tall fireplace was the main feature of this room, it too had a fender one could park your bottom on. Two leathers winged back chair were at right angles to the fireplace each having a small wooden table covered by an embroidered linen cloth. That said simply EG she assumed that must have been the lady who made these. A long leather couch was not that far away with two folded blankets hung over the end. Plenty of cushions made this look extremely comfortable. Other tables were around with flowers or Eileen could envisage laying on that couch reading. The walls had paintings hung in straight lines. All of them signed DG Above the fire was a large plaque that said Gaunt on it was she assumed the family crest, it had the picture of eagle's claws, holding large rabbit. It was designed like a shield, with a mustard type yellow and a rustic red.

"My name is Sir Frederick William John Gaunt the master of Lysham Manor and you are? "

"Oh yes Miss Eileen Mason Perry Sir. But I prefers to be called just Elle"

The mystery of Lysham Manor by NanyWytch

"Well pleased to make your acquaintance, he offered her a small brandy saying drink it down will take the chill out your bones. So, might I call you Eileen or Miss Perry."

"Eileen or Elle will be fine Miss Perry sounds very formal."

Sir Fredrick says after we have eaten you could take a bath if you desire before retiring unless like me you are exhausted tonight.' Leah came in carrying a tray with broth and chunks of bread a butter dish and cutlery wrapped in linen serviette. A young man carried the tea tray they just placed them down and the man said "would you like me to pour the tea Sir,"

"Oh no Edward, I think we are quite capable of that"

Leah re-entered the room carrying a plate full of slices of the most lemon scented cake. Eileen had ever smelt the flavour drifted up her nose as Leah past her. The broth was ridiculously hot and so full of vegetables it was thick and smelt of beef. Chunks of meat were cooked so well they melted in contact with the tongue.

"Leah I am unsure which room was given to Eileen will you make sure she is placed in my wife's old room. "

"Are you sure Sir it's not been cleaned for a while maybe we can put her in the east wing in the room with the rounded window it gets good light Sir, "

"Yes, ok get a fire laid and can you find out if she might take a bath as well? Go into my wife's things get out a nightdress and robe please Leah. "

"Of course, Sir. "

The mystery of Lysham Manor by NanyWytch

The servants were gone the door closed."

"Sir you ought not go to so much trouble for me' says Elle

"It is no trouble lass in fact to have some company is lovely. There are no men about my home as my sons are away at Eton. I have two sons John the eldest he is a hateful boy, he is obstinate cruel and forever hurting his brother Daniel who is so vastly different he is quiet, very artistic most of the paintings in here are his. Their mother died when they were so ridiculously small so without a mother, I have spoilt them giving John as the elder boy far too much leeway. John was but 10 his younger brother but 7 years old a succession of nanny's took care of them which is no substitute for a mother who loved them both dearly, I miss her so much even today now 10 years since she passed away. "

"So, do tell me more about whom your aunt was?"

"She was my only relative, so I am now all alone in the world, her cottage is all locked up. They said you might have keys here as you own her property. I arrived far too late and have no idea if she had a will, all I know is she wrote to me saying she was sick and to come as soon as possible. It has taken me 8 days Sir as I walked most of the way saving my money for lodging at night. Now I have but eight pennies to my name the lawyer is not back for some 3 to 4 days they said. At the office earlier. The priest in the church said Ivy mill might have work so I walked there this afternoon but all the jobs were gone "

The mystery of Lysham Manor by NanyWytch

Fredrick listened to her explaining her predicaments. He said' "let me look if we do have a set of keys."

Looking in the desk he mutters to himself. "Are you ok Sir" Elle asks him? 'Yes, I was just thinking maybe my steward has the keys unless we gave ours to the lawyers. I can check in the morning. "

"Without work I would have nothing to pay lawyers with Sir, which was why I asked if you needed a maid Sir. That I might earn monies to sort out my aunt's cottage, so I am not left destitute at your door."

"Well Eileen as you can see, I do have staff that care very well for me, what I do need however is a companion who is well educated, can read and write of course whom can help me catalogue the books in the library. I do need other help too my wife used keep the household accounts and help with the accounts for the estate. I can teach you how to do this my fingers are a bit old now not so nimble as yours. "Fredrick explains his offer.

"What about your son John when he is home will he not help you?" Says Eileen

"Fredrick laughs argh my son, my precious eldest boy. No, my dear he is far too aggressive handling books is not in his nature. Gambling getting wasted and riding are his passions. I gave him far too much of his own way after their mother died. I felt obliged make it better. I doubt John will do anything about the land I wish he would as the direct air. Daniel he's not interested in the farming side, but he does love decorating the house & painting. He is like his mother far too gentle and soft centred so much so his brother bullies him."

"Sir I can read and write am well, acquainted with books, Sir my parents owned a book shop prior to their demise. Plus, I think you need some company who can help you manage things here it must be exceedingly difficult at times you must feel lonely in a big place like this."

"Yes, you would think not with all the servants 26 of them we have here, it would not be possible but most of my friends live 5 miles from here in Haworth. So yes, I miss my Izzy. The servants keep out of my way as is the custom unless summoned so young lady is it a, yes? Yes, Sir I would like the position please and fully accept your offer of help with my aunt's estate I had no idea how to progress being a woman I was not used to dealing with lawyers myself Sir."

"In that case it pays £15 per year with board & lodging of course and you get two days off per month. Sundays are free of course except for attending church with me. All my staff attend morning Mass. Are you roman Catholic or this new-fangled Methodism I heard of? Or God forbid this table rapping nonsense sweeping the nation. With talking boards."

"No Sir I attend mass is it in Latin or English? oh it is in Latin I will give you a prayer book. It is alright sir I have my mother's which is why I asked if the priest conducts mass in Latin. my parents were from Italy but came to England just after I was born, we lived in Devon So, you are a few miles from home then. Well, if you will, have me this could become my home. I

The mystery of Lysham Manor by NanyWytch

do have another question Sir would I as your companion be eating with the servants or yourself."

"Awe good question lass, Ermm let me decide that tomorrow its rather late now if you want a bath and a good sleep Leah will have it already pull that cord near the fire for me save my legs. Of course, Sir. "

Leah came you rang Sir, "yes Leah is the room ready and can our guest have a hot bath?"

"Yes, Sir cooks boiled the water it will be ready in a few minutes, if that is OK will there be anything more tonight Sir."

"No thank you Leah, you can tell the staff they may go to bed as soon as I am settled, I am sure Elle will be happy see to herself."

 Yes Sir of course Sir I will send Edward to you help you Sir, would you like any hot chocolate tonight oh yes with a tot of brandy my dear. Offer Eileen some too we do not want her having a fever."

"Of course, Sir I will send it up with Edward."

"Thank you, Leah."

Eileen bids him goodnight and follows Leah to the room in the east wing. The room is beautifully decorated the fire so cosy the flicker of the logs dances about the room there is two candle sticks on the dresser near the window. The bed is this huge four posters with these angels carved into the headboard. The large chest at the bed base has a cushion on it to sit on, in the huge window are more cushions one could dream inside that window behind the thick brocade curtains. Leah had two men bring the bath into the room then fill it with jugs of hot water handing Eileen some lavender and rose petals to scent the water and some soap that smelt of roses. Eileen said thank you Leah told her about the hot chocolate coming in around 30 minutes. Eileen undressed then sank into that hot water, it felt so good her feet were filthy, good job they gave her sponges. Her legs up to her knees had now got baked in mud on them, she asked Leah about her clothes from before. Leah said" they had been washed and were drying in the kitchen. They would be ironed in the morning after the fires were lit."

"Thank you so much Leah. "

Eileen sang to herself whilst in bath thinking how lucky she was to have been invited into such a house. She had imagined being handed a blanket to sleep near the kitchen fire Her thoughts drifted to before she had left her home a quiet country house that compared to this was small, even though it had six bedrooms two sitting rooms plus rooms for servants above this not forgetting fathers' study and the library, she had been very comfortable there, but being without a fortune and only £2,000 per year inheritance that had been invested till she was 25 she was not considered a good catch for a gentleman. Plus, she had not been introduced to society without family to help her. She had only her aunt whom she was hoping might push her into the path of a handsome husband. However, life was not going to do so now her aunt was gone, Sir Fredrick said he would speak with his lawyer on the morrow to enquire for her about her aunts' home and money. With his help she might still, find a gentleman to ensure she would not spend her life alone. She had gone through some serious shifts in finances over the years. She had learnt about hunger, pestilence, child birth, in the workhouse. The matron had her writing reports for her, filling in forms. Then helping out with any women about to birth a child. So, our Elle had seen them born, seen them die, seen them starve, or ill. The only reason she was in the women's section was that she could read and write very well indeed. She was very useful have around. The matron could not read nor write.

Eileen wondered what it would have been like to be born into a family like this. Live here in such a big house she had only seen a few rooms so far, she wanted explore but that would be rude she wondered what the sons looked like seeing pictures along the hall there were some very old ones plus some newer ones. Leah knocked at the door Eileen was now out of the water wrapped into a towelling robe. Leah laid out new under garments for the morning plus she had this red satin gown and these red pumps that had this amazingly simple rose embroidered on the top. Eileen said

"Is this for me"

"Yes, the master sent it for you said it ought to fit you. Here is a night dress for tonight miss. "

"Thank you so much Leah, will, you thank the master too please. He has retired for the night miss maybe you can do that at breakfast. "

Might the men remove the tub miss before you retire? Of course, Leah I do not wish to be a bother. It is our job miss to follow the master's orders take care of this place and him"

"Of course, good night" Leah.

I will fetch your hot chocolate miss

"Oh, Leah is there any of that cake left do you think I might have a slice please"

"Of course, miss anything else."

"Oh no thank you. "

Leah left the room goes to the kitchen says to cook.

"She only wants more cake as well. Greedy pig she demolished that soup and bread ate, half that cake as we know the master only eats a couple of your thick slices at best. What will she be eating for breakfast half the larder? Mentions Leah Saying

Mary might be right she could be a witch she said she knows anti gossip spells to sew your mouth shut Mary,"

"Leah she is the master's guest so keep your thoughts to yourself you know nothing about the girl as yet. She might have been very hungry." Says Sarah the cook

"I know she arrived here sodden wet looking like a tramp mud halfway up that dress and my god mud on her undress and her stocking were grey not white." Moans Mary

Leah," please take the tray upstairs then go to bed"

"Yes, cook, what will Henry think when he comes back."

"You do not know if he is coming back girl to bed with thee."

The next day she dressed with the help of Leah, going down to breakfast being told she was joining the master in the breakfast room to eat with him.

After breakfast, the master asked for the staff to come to the hall, they arrived wondering what was going on. Master Fredrick said this is miss Eileen Mason Perry she has been employed as my companion as such her time will be very much with me. Therefore, you will treat her as if she were a guest rather than another servant is that clear"

"Yes, Sir they say"

"You are dismissed go about your work;"

Edward leaves grumbling about this girl being treated like family not servant but getting paid too.

"Edward shut up shouts the Cook, none of your business how the master decides do things"

"Well just saying master John will be back for Christmas and master Daniel do you think they will stand for it. "Grumbles Edward

"Until master John is our master, he will have to abide by his father's wishes Sir Fredrick is no weaklings be bossed around by his sons. "Says Sarah Edward keeps up his protesting

"Just saying they will not like it is all. She is not even high class she is more like us her parents were in trade after all."

"Edward enough do you not have boots to clean" shouts Sarah

"I am going, stop bossing me about you are not Henry"

"I am the cook and if you want feeding lad. I would shift your arse out of my kitchen "

she waves her wooden spoon at the lad. Tutting "Leah those carrots will not cut themselves, "

"But I am not the scullery maid, "

"Leah just do its Sarah is sick in bed, I need the vegetables cut up."

"Mary is Lower than me get her to do it, I have to go clean upstairs"

"I do not care which one does it as long as it is done, but I am ironing the washing and her clothing. "

For god's sake I am glad Henry will be here today after his week visiting his mother. Things will get back to normal in this place he will not stand for all this back talking."

"Hey, get your dirty boots off my clean floor, "cook says to the gardener

"But I need a cuppa" say's Symons

"Get them boots off then you can have your tea it is in the pot." Says Sarah smiling at him.

"OK miss bossy boots satisfied" wiggles his tongue at her in fun.

"No stay out my way till lunch time this kitchen my domain not yours you belong into garden"

The mystery of Lysham Manor by NanyWytch

"Oh yes mistress and he bow, saying we are not worthy of thy fine wares madam." Taunting her laughing the cook slaps him with her spoon,

"Get away with thee."

Symons joked about with Sarah they had both grown up here.
"

Any chance of some biscuit's fair maiden.?"

"In the tin, thank-you."

He takes his mug sits by the fire warming his legs. The smell comes off his warmer socks, it's, ripe.

"My god Symons can thee change the socks; they reek"

"Make me more tea I will do it."

"There are clean dry ones in the laundry room."

Yes, mistress he says Munching on biscuits made yesterday.

"Do not you take all day."

"Yes, fair mistress" mocks the gardener be off we thee. He runs out the door puts his new socks on then his boots on outside.

Meanwhile Sir Fredrick is showing Eileen around outside as they are walking, they talked about her aunt and his two sons, he showed her the outside of the house. As they walked Sir Fredrick said now tell me about your family in Devon.

"What area are you from and who exactly is Elle."

The mystery of Lysham Manor by NanyWytch

"Well Sir it's a sad tale to be sure, they sat in the garden.

"Marshall, will you go tell Leah we are to have our coffee here."

"Of course, Sir, wonderful that lad has been a blessing he is a lot nicer than my own boys I must admit. "

They sat in the sun; it was a very nice garden." Elle said when I was young, we lived in a very fine house with 4 servants, Emma was my maid but in truth she was more like a mother to me. My own mother was always out at some other person's house. I hardly saw her. My father had this business in town. We lived in Cloverlly. however, my father came home one night said his investments had gone bad and he had lost it all. I didn't understand mother cried; father went to his study moments later he shot himself. I ran there at the bang; his brains decorated the wall behind him and part of his face was on the floor blood was everywhere. But I still kissed his other cheek. Two days later my mother took her life in her room bleeding out on the silk rug. Emma said I wasn't to upset myself too much the lawyers will sort it all out. Everything will be ok. But when my Uncle Thomas came, he said there were a lot of debts so the only way forward was to auction off the house land and contents.

Maybe some monies will be left. He told me he loved me as his niece but I could not live with them as his house was far too small As well as over crowded with his three children So, I had no idea what was actually occurring I was only 7 years old Sir. On the auction day I saw our neighbours, the very same

The mystery of Lysham Manor by NanyWytch

ones who had come to dinner parties or dances here. They looked down their noses at me so I told Emma they were like Carrion sticking their beaks into everything looking for a meal. They feasted on all our things which had been tagged with prices. I ran to my mother's room took her jewellery took my father's fob watch and his rings. I took my mother's small Latin prayer book. My Greek and Latin book my China tea set, my China faced doll. Plus, my ragga Anny we made together from scraps.

I hid it in the tree house no adult can get inside there. I sat there eating my sandwich drinking my milk Emma had fetched me. She said we ought to sew the gold into my coat for later as emergency fund. She helped me do that in the kitchens. Margaret the Cook was so cuddly to lean onto I think in those days I knew the servants better than my parents.

The house was so totally bare without our things inside it. I found some money in fathers' desk so paid the butcher, greengrocer, the staff, and had £1 left over. The lawyer sat me down in the kitchen whilst drinking tea having some chocolate cake. He explained to the staff that today was there last day. To me he said your father put some money aside for when you are 21 years old. There is nothing for it you will go to the workhouse. I asked what it was Emma said its where people go who don't have any money. The lawyer took me there, but I had walk into the place on my own. The mistress was a huge woman, she took my clothes put them into a box with my name on it. Saying you get them back when you leave here. I didn't get my gold back they took it. At 8 years old I was sold to the mill for £5 along with four others. Singleton's mill had five floors the top floor housed us to sleep in full of beds it was two to a bed. The master said as I could read and write knew Latin and Greek, I could work at the big house help his wife with the ledgers keep her company. She dressed me in better clothes when visitors came, she told them she adored me. Truth was she hated me for being there, even though I knew etiquette her guest thought my lovely. Her son was very mean to me kicking me biting me called my paupers brat and other things one day I had just had enough of his bullying, so I burst his nose kicked him sat on him pinching his ribs he screamed for his mother who was out. His father came from out the study, picked me up by the waist said now as I do not keep a zoo who is going to tell me what is going on here. He put me down. I told him his son was a mindless bully deserved my hitting him. He slapped his son on the head said he had heard this before but this was too far he was sending him boarding school. He said I was going work in the mill.

"So, Elle you learnt money can vanish in a minute, you learnt to work hard, get on with your life."

"Yes, sir it's the only place I have worked" Did the mill Master know how far you were going?"

"Yes, he did he slipped an extra couple of pounds said shhh it never happened folk will think me soft"

They started to walk again Sir Fredrick was talking about the house as he was showing her the outside.

 he was explaining which rooms were the newest ones. It seemed to have a lot of rooms seeing the house in daylight it looked larger with the tiny windows of the top floor. He pointed to the round tower room's saying his wife, loved these rooms had her very own sitting room in one of them. The drawing room in the other. She used the sitting room for writing her letters, doing menus, going through household accounts she was an excellent wife and mother. He said he would show her the inside after lunch saying during the work, they could shut themselves up in the library start on the books. He said it costs quiet a lot of money keep this place running right now its running very well we grow most of our grains here barley, wheat, Rye we make our own butter and cheeses have a small orchard for apples that is made into cider sold at the Black bull have you been there on your way here?

"No Sir I do not really like going in taverns had to on the way here there are some nasty ones with extremely poor food that cost six pennies for a room, then two for stew, then one penny for pint of warm ale. So, I did not have enough and did not want risk my last pennies drinking warm ale without anywhere to change my clothes. "

"Well, you would have been safe there William the owner is a good man plus this being the north a room costs 6d with food and ale thrown in. So, you might have stayed there."

"Well Sir thank you maybe one day you might escort me there. Being a lady, I much prefer not to go into places full of drunken men alone."

"Did you know that you might have met the Reverend son in there he lives in there most days sits in corner at back near the fire? You will meet them Sunday anyway his daughters can advise us about your aunt. Daughter she said oh yes, he has three lovely ones but I prefers Emily myself she's more relaxed than the others get on with her brother more. I will introduce you so that you will at least know some females. Actually, we do need go into Haworth later I want buy some paper and tea this shops half way down the hill. Oh yes, I stopped there to rest on way up it had lots of different flavours. Is it not expensive for tea? Yes, can buy pint a gin cheaper lass. Maybe I can take you try food in the black bull."

"Oh, Sir that would be lovely. I need my other shoes repaired"

"Yes, we can buy decent boots down the hill the ironmongers have things hung outside old Thomas is a nice chap lost his wife and boys to typhoid poor man in fact a lot of people died from it last year.

That evening dinner was arranged for 8pm the master had invited guests to meet this young lady he now had to accompany him keep him fit. The guests arrived at 7.30pm for drinks. Amongst them was the lawyer to Sir Fredrick and his family, plus the Dr and then two ladies of society to balance out the table they were sisters. Lady fair Hurst and her sister asked Eileen where she was from? She replies a small village in the Devon since the mills came the place has grown experientially. The mill owners have built a school and houses on the hill at the other side of the original village. But the folk of the original village have nothing to do with the Irish moving in after the famine they had."

"Have you been introduced to society, yet you look so young?"

"No ma'am I was to go with my aunt, but she had become ill she died before I arrived, we planned go to Buxton to the big winter house."

The mystery of Lysham Manor by NanyWytch

"I have been there a fine place many shops. Fredrick says you were caught in that storm last evening your poor girl how old did you say you were."

"I did not but I am 18 now. "Do you dance or sing or indeed play music?"

"I sing a lot but am not particularly good singing for others. I dance but I did not learn to play the harpsichord yet"

"Well, we can help you as two spinsters we have plenty of time on our hands I am lady Katina Elizabeth Fair Hurst my sister is Susanna Joan Fair Hurst we live in the village now, unfortunately our brother demanded we moved out when he inherited our home in Holden,"

Come sister shall, we talk to the other, They walk away from Eileen she had not expected to be interrogated she felt intimidated when her parents were alive, she was classed as being an upper middle-class female but there were debts the house sold, she ended up being sold to the mill owner to work for free. So right now, she could not hold her own properly with these upper-class females who think of nothing but entertaining themselves, when she had ended up so extremely poor. It is a big shock to one day be a well to do person the next end up at the workhouse. She had come to know how it really feels not knowing when you will eat next.

The dining room was in a more classical design painted a pale green colour; it had a huge dining table in the centre. The big house keeper's mahogany sideboard against the rear wall. The fireplace was in the same style as the other main rooms. A crystal candelabra held 12 candles above the dining table set out with Berwick pottery all genuinely nice made in Staffordshire known as the pot banks. She had been here with her parents to a mill watched a worker make rose petals brooches from China clay. She loved Daulton pottery her mother had bought on that trip sadly it had been auctioned off with everything else. As a child she thought the neighbours who attended the auction were like crows sticking their beaks into every small item acting greedy to save a few shillings. Expecting things to go cheaply that day they were wrong. Being only 10 she had taken a book from the library about history and a Greek textbook, mothers Latin prayer book. she wanted the family bible, but her aunt took that home with her. Eileen had hidden in the tree house her father had built she packed her small China dolls tea set into her rucksack so nobody else got to playhouse with it. she had taken just one doll with her and her diary. But at the workhouse the matron took them off her even her two gold chains and locket from her parent. She never saw them again. Thinks they sold her gold and her China doll.

In the kitchen cook was getting a bit flustered about the meal as it was such short notice to do a meal for six. However, as the larder was well stocked and the game keeper dropped in a duck and a goose plus three rabbits, they were not short of meats. She made up a rabbit pie, for the staff's dinner and the goose for upstairs, dinner went down well then, they had some music and dancing as the Dr was good at playing the fiddle a small secret, he kept from most but as Fredrick had known him a long time, he knew about it.

The mystery of Lysham Manor by NanyWytch

The next day's Mary came in with the tea tray at 9am, to wake Eileen she was quiet upset saying that the master was found earlier not being able to breathe properly he had taken an early morning stroll as always before breakfast but Marshall Roche had found him on the ground. The Dr had been sent for; Eileen rushed into the red dress that had been given her from his wife's collection. She drank her tea as fast as she could scooped up her hair clipping it into a pile onto her head with Mary's help. Then went downstairs into the drawing room to find him sitting in a chair near the fire, covered in a blanket. His breathing was a bit laboured, but he said

"It had happened before that maybe last night had tired him out more than he had thought as he had not had so much fun in ages"

"Eileen asked if she might look about the rooms whilst he rested yes of course dear please do best get find your way around." She had seen the bells on the wall of the kitchen all labelled up. Drawing room, library, billiard room, study, master bedroom, lady's room, panelled room, 6 more bedrooms, ballroom, art room, plus servants' rooms, stables gamekeeper's cottage, boot room, scullery, kitchen, laundry room, back stairs, cooks sitting room, butlers' room, pantry, dry storage room, cellar, drying room. Boot room gun room. The place sounded like a maze. It would take time teach her way around as a night the music room, dining room, billiard room were used. During the day morning room, library study, and the drawing room. It would take time teach her way around here.

Eileen was overly concerned about him, the Dr came in and within minutes he knew what was wrong it appeared he had a chest infection too much snuff the Dr said, too much excitement. He prescribed something help him sleep, plus suggested warm honey and lemon drinks. Fredrick said "

with whiskey in them."

Dr said "you need cut your drinking down, not increase it."

"Impossible says Fredrick it is my only vices along with my snuff."

"I know you do not forget a few tipples in the day, then more at night."

"It keeps me sane. If a man cannot relax inside his own home we are stuffed"

"Maybe so but now you have someone to converse with you ought to be much better I am sure she can pamper you very well. The Dr bids him good day. Then tells Eileen to make sure he rests; she says she will do everything she can to help him.

That night Marshall Roche sat up with the master to make sure he was OK. In the morning Eileen went to see him propped up in his bed. He was drinking tea, but his eyes were heavy from lack of sleep he had been coughing a lot of the night.

Fredrick said to Marshall" go to bed lad, you look all in. "

"Thank you Sir I will after breakfast,"

Fredrick said" that lad has done more for me than my two sons".

The mystery of Lysham Manor by NanyWytch

She asked if he were hungry wanted try some food saying she would go fetch a tray for him.

"He nodded yes eggs on toast please with more tea. Do not forget your own breakfast lass. "

She went to the kitchen it was a hive of activity, Sarah the cook was scrambling eggs, Leah scrubbing pans, Mary was polishing silver. Marshall was wolfing down bacon and eggs with hunk of bread slurping on his tea. An older man dozed in a chair near the fire.

Sarah says "that's the master's tray what would you like to eat there is bacon and eggs or kippers".

"Oh, bacon and egg toast and tea will be fine. I can wait for it."

"No ma'am you take the masters tray I will send Leah up with yours, if you are sitting with the master watch over him."

Yes, I said I would so Marshall could go bed.

"I will make a nice soup for lunch miss."

"Anything you normally do is fine by me; I am hoping that the master might get some sleep"

"Did the Dr not leave something yesterday,"

"Yes, but he refused take any"

"Oh, he is a stubborn man you will get used to him. Tis a wonder he is still in his bed, he is normally up and about by 6am wandering gardens talking to our Symons over there in the chair. "

As Eileen got to the master's room with the tray he was up and dressed.

"Sir you ought to be resting you looked so tired. Bless your heart girl I would much rather be in the library than wasting time in bed we can get on with sorting the books.

"I will get Marshall in here to lift down the heavy ones later but if we start on the lower shelves, it will be fine"

"Sir I do not know if they have been dusted yet the Dr said it would make your chest worse."

"Fiddlesticks he just frets about the small stuff. It is my body my life so I will decide what to do, so no more but Sirs I said no more Elle hush! "

he took the cord pulled it to tell them they were to eat in the breakfast room far more respectable than cooped up in bed.

"Now I was going to show you around the manor today but like you said my chest is a bit wheezy so instead we will go look at the plans I have for the west wing. However, before we descend those stairs there is something, I want to show you. Come along we are only going down here to what was my wife's room"

. Sir Fredrick opened the door to the room, sun shone brightly through the corner window. He opened the thick brocade red curtains to light up the whole room. A portrait took pride of place above the fireplace, it was this lovely lady in a blue gown with emerald eyes holding roses. She had her hair draped over one shoulder it was a golden-brown colour like wheat.

The mystery of Lysham Manor by NanyWytch

Fredrick said "this was lily his wife that it was painted not long after she had come as his bride." He opened the large wardrobe which to Eileen's surprise was full of dresses, shoes, cloaks. Elle gasped as he pulled out this embroidered purple evening gown saying this was her wedding gown.

"The other gowns were made for our daughter; she spent her time sewing clothes for every age whilst she was pregnant. But as you know she died giving birth almost 10years ago now. I simply could not justify parting with her things just the smell reminds me of my Izzy, I loved her so very much, but you need some clothes suitable to your new standing of a person of property. So young lady you might as well choose some of these to have in your room. In those draws over there are my wife's linens and other garments women wear so I will ask Leah bring some to your room. On that dresser are the glass perfume bottles and bowl for talc and such like. Plus, I would like give you something your neck looked very bare at our dinner. So, I picked this from my wife's things it just a small trinket nothing too much to grace your tiny neck. He placed a box in her hand she opened it and she said no I cannot take this it is far too much Sir. No arguments will be had its my gift to you, my girl. So, let us place it about your neck. It is a shame it has not been out the box for ten years I just could not get rid of her things which is why you were lucky as regards female attire. He tied the silk ribbon and the amethyst stone hung lovely on her. Now look at that would you believe it makes your eyes more vibrant and alive come child our coffee will be coming soon. I told Leah take it to the drawing room. "

"How can I ever repay you for the kindness you have shown me since yesterday? "

"There is only one way to repay kindness my girl it is with kindness itself."

The mystery of Lysham Manor by NanyWytch

Chapter Three Illness creeps in

Over the next six months Sir Fredrick seemed to be getting stronger. They strolled the gardens Fredrick introduced her to Symons the gardener, saying

"This is my companion, Eileen; you have done a mighty fine job on the gardens this year." Symons touched his old, battered trilby hat at the master,

"Thank-you Sir tis my greatest pleasure this garden. I do not think I am doing so bad for sixty-two though. I think I might be good for a few years yet"

He smiles showing his brown teeth. Symons had grown up here as a lad he had played with Sir Fredrick it felt odd to him calling his best friend Master. Symons had learnt the trade from his own father who worked for the family some 40 years. He had worked since being 14 years old as apprentice gardener then been promoted till, he was head gardener only one have an outbuilding with a heater and chair rest in. So, now he had worked 48 years nearly did not feel that long because he loved his job very many flowers were a passion for him.

He took her to the stables see Marshall Roche,

"He has been here now some six years now, he does all the odd jobs as well, as tends the horses. This way I keep the costs down you see. Running a large estate as this can cost a lot of money, we are lucky as we have the farm producing much of our grains and meat, eggs, cheese, butter and milk is all produced here. We have a few labourers live over there in those small cottages and at harvest time everyone mucks in."

He asks how Marshall is,

"I be fine Sir, tis good see you thriving again too."

"Yeah, it is that is this young lady who has been taking great care of me these past months"

Eileen helps Fredrick catalogue the library which took several weeks of daily work, the books seemed endless. By now she had been there some 8 months it had flown by her thought the laughing at his silly jokes made the day lovely. Leah dusted the shelves humming to herself indeed the house was an incredibly happy one. Their conversations seemed endless as Christmas was coming on faster than one would want, Fredrick talked about his sons coming back for the holidays. Then without warning Fredrick suffered a small heart attack he survived but was very weak and this time he stayed to his bed. Eileen tended his every whim and prevented him getting up several times. One day after two weeks of him being in bed a letter arrived Fredrick was too weak to read it, so Eileen read it him.

9th January 1855

My dearest papa

We are sorry we did not make the yuletide with you, however we landed in London on the 7th. We intend to visit you in the near future. Father, John has not been too well, but his heavy drinking does not bode well, or his tendency for the card table. Not you mention whores. There is no need to meet us we are having the axle repaired to our carriage. John gambled our horse in a card game. So, we had to buy another one he charged it to your account Sir,

Love

Daniel.

"So, they are back from Eton are they along with swanning about England visiting friends, plus having the nerve charge their account to me. They both get quite a substantial allowance from me per month keep them to a high standard of living. No doubt they have charged the hotels and liquor bill to me with a few loose women added in on top. They are downright rogues the pair of them"

Sir Fredrick was almost purple with rage.

"Please Sir calm down I expect they do still. Love you very much you should be pleased you are getting to see them.

"They do not know the meaning of the word, so why would they change the path they are on for me. They put their mother in her grave and they will put me in mine but no more I will not have him squandering this estate into the ground. It has been in our family a long time, but he is such a moron."

He fell back onto the pillows exhausted it was very apparent that letter upset him a lot. She was worried about him having another attack. After he was sleeping, she went down to the kitchens talk to the staff. They told Elle if the master died, they would not want remain working there under master John.

The mystery of Lysham Manor by NanyWytch

The following week Sir Fredrick had a relapse the Dr said he needed write to the hotel in London ordering his sons to come home. Fredrick objected said no it is not happening I will not condone it. The Dr said then I will write to them you will do no such thing do you hear me. Listen to me they need to be told you are unwell, fiddlesticks they can find out when they come from London begging for more money.

The next day Fredrick was worse so Eileen persuaded him to dictate a letter to go to London so if he got even worse, they would be there. He agreed under protest, so a letter was sent

Dear John & Daniel

You are to come home immediately, your father is seriously ill, I have sent monies to pay for the axle and horse make sure you pay them and the hotel prior to leaving.

DR Stroud

The mystery of Lysham Manor by NanyWytch

Chapter 4 Homecoming

On receipt of the letter in the hotel room John laughed, so papa is sick maybe he will die soon then the manor will be mine. He wanders around rubbing his hands in glee all mine, all mine I will finally be the Master of the estate. The things I will change dear brother.

'Are we to leave today dear brother says Daniel' John replies dancing about like a fool. 'No I have a few things I needs to do, couple of days maybe.'

'John father could be dying surely you grasped this from this letter, the Dr signed it not our father'. Don't fret little lamb you will be well cared for always my dear baby brother.'

'Is that so John as your drinking & gambling spread like a fever in your brain' Daniel relax when are you going to open your eyes, look at these wenches, come on do they not entice you at all. Do you want a boy instead brother?' 'Hell, no I do not '

"Daniel yelled at him as he was swinging the brandy from the bottle. 'Come on John let us leave early then tomorrow '

Danny boy John danced about him laughing "come on take these two wenches to thy bed and use your dick for what it meant for screwing them silly. What do you say brother of mine"?

John swigs more brandy from the bottle sinking his face into a girl's breasts? Who reminds him she isn't free, holds her hand out for coin John places coins into her hand says 'her as well?' She whispers into his ear, 'she is a kinky whore, are you sure you want to play this game'. "Hel, yes wench how much for her as well another 2 shilling. He hands over the money.

'Come my brother has not yet decided to use his dick for something other than pissing into a pot.'

Daniel takes a carafe of wine to his room, knowing his brother is as senseless as the ducks in the pond with drink on him. He hears his brother yelling and swearing in the next room, then the squeals of delight, girls laughing as he pours brandy down their throats. Adding strawberries and cream to their ripened bodies to lick off them. To John this was better than desert he was in ecstasy unfolded between their thighs one with his dick the other with his mouth.

The next morning Daniel walks into Johns room to wake him up it's gone 11am 'get up you lazy drunken skunk. Come on I have things to do', John wraps his fingers in the girl's hair slaps her arse saying 'later now go my brother wishes me out if this sweaty pit.' John lounges in the bed running his fingers over his curly hair. 'Come now what is more important than testing out your prowess away from home'. Daniel did not take the bait he says 'are you going to wash and get up or am I to do the shopping for both of us.'

'What shopping says John?'

'The gifts of course our clothing we ordered the fitting is in an hour come on wash dress let's go.'

'Daniel, have you taken wine with breakfast and not small ale? You are very forward.'

The mystery of Lysham Manor by NanyWytch

"Of course, I am I wish to see my father and see him alive, if you do not mind so come on out of the bed."

John grabs his arm pulling him onto the bed. Then he sits over him, naked Daniel says "John it's one thing dangling that monster over girls. Not me please brother have one of my own you know so get off me "

'Well, there was last night swearing you were playing in the other league. I didn't think a dick would make you cringe away. So, it is wenches then you like?'

'Of course, its is'. 'Then you can take Hazel she is a fine filly ripe indeed for you to take the haunches with'

"John wash dress it's nearly noon."

"Oh yes he yawns outside go outside today I don't you think so the sun is rather bright through those drapes do me the honour of closing them I got no sleep. So, I am not for town but for sleep go without me we will meet for dinner later."

Daniel shakes his head "your brain is addled still from drink but I will get our things as you laze, away the day."

John vanishes under the blankets is snoring before Daniel leaves the room, he thinks to himself when he is master, he cannot play this game he must manage the estate.

Daniel knew his brother was made of different stuff, his sense of entitlement for one. Plus, his gambling & drinking were not under control. He did not realise he was not behaving well for a highly educated gentleman. Daniel just hopes he pays the bills before we leave this time. Father would not be pleased if he didn't. The next day Daniel asks John should we not go home today? No says John we are going the market,

Daniel doesn't mind this because he wishes to buy gifts to take home as they missed Christmas. At market Daniel was with John for the fitting of his new coat in purple silk. Then he picked a silk waistcoat for father in a nice cream. He asked his brother if he wanted something here to which Daniel said no. They went out from the fitters around the market, Daniel reminds him they need gifts for the servants too as they missed seeing them at Christmas John said" what the hell don't, we pay them enough."

Daniel bought the gifts himself as John walked into the Tavern "meet me in here, he says we will eat lunch together."

Daniel nods them continues his shopping he purchases a necklace for Leah & Mary then a metal sign saying best cook in the world for Sarah. He buys a nice linen shirt for his father, a linen waistcoat for Marshall, a Scarf for Edward then Symons gets a trowel with his name engraved on it. Once he has been the art shop for oils and new brushes linseed oil a few charcoal pieces plus new canvas and art paper. He is ready to eat so goes to meet John. Who was half cut from the bottle of brandy he had asked for?

"Daniel says I do hope you are going to eat with that"

"Awe my dear brother yes I am starving, I missed breakfast." They ask for ham cheese bread and pickles. They are brought two platters plus another glass for the brandy. Daniel asks for small ale. They enjoy their lunch Daniel asks John is he coming back to the other side of London with him as the carriage is ready. "No I think I might play cards."

"John come back with me now please."

"Daniel leaves me alone go if you want I will see you later. "

Daniel leaves returning to their hotel, he relaxes with a good book near the fire. John does not return till the early hours of the morning falling down drunk. The staff had to carry him upto his room he slept fully clothed.

The next day Daniel plans to leave he drags his brother out of bed screaming his head hurt protesting loudly at being woken. Daniel asks the hotel if the bill was settled, they told him it had been charged to his father by his older brother. Along with all other debts. Daniel enquires what debts? The axle the horse plus gambling debts he ran up here. Daniel apologises to them says my father will be in contact when were they sent! Yesterday he was told.

He dragged his brother kicking and screaming into the carriage hands him water John pushes It away takes out his hip flask drinks brandy

'

Two days later the sons arrived without warning, the coach pulled up outside. The servants were prepared as they had cleaned the rooms already and had kept the place tidy.

The mystery of Lysham Manor by NanyWytch

The first to disembark was John the eldest, he saw all the normal staff then stared long and hard at Eileen." Who the deuce is you?" He snarled.

"I Sir am your father companion miss Eileen Mason Perry; you I take it are his eldest son, John."

"Correct now get my bags taken to my room"

Eileen retorts "If you wish your bags taken to your room might, I suggest you carry them yourself because I will leave them right here.

I have been tending your father during these past months. I am a guest here'. John placed his hand under her chin '

"Spirit is fine in a horse but in a wench, it can be broken quickly. You get paid from the estate wench, so you are a servant. I will be addressed as Master John by you, Marshall takes the bags,"

"Yes, Sir right away Sir."

"Now that's how servants behave you ought to take lessons. Says John in front of everyone

"I am not a servant here," Eileen shouted at him

'John retorts moving right upto her face. You get £15 per year from this estate which makes you a servant. So, its master John to you. Get out of my way wench".

Mary smirked; John snarled at her making her cringe he was well known for going with the last under house maid getting her pregnant which his father had to deal with. Just as he was

The mystery of Lysham Manor by NanyWytch

well known for his bad manners, attitude he was better than anyone else here.

Eileen said "If you wish to see your father he is resting right now,"

" I will see him when I deem it necessary and not before first I am going riding " says John "

"Then Sir I consider you a selfish pig, your father could be dying and yet you care more for the brandy than him"

"Oh, do shut up its rather boring you know listening to you drone on. Oh, by the way its master John to you as your just a servant"

He empathised the word Servant louder than the rest of the words He smirked at her in his way he did like her for actually standing up to him, nobody had ever done this before so it was something of a surprise, he needed play on this find out more.

"Now we are home you can eat in the kitchens; where you belong, we do not have servants at our dining table."

"I will not she yells' He smirked at her. Then eat outside just not at my table. Servant! "

She could see from his behaviours they were not going to get along. But Eileen had dealt with worse at the mill back in Devon

Eileen said "I think it is up to your father not you as he is master here, I do believe sir"

"Oh, servant I will be altering things around here you eat with the servants, I do not want you at my table the affairs of the family are nothing to do with you. The next time you address me its master John or Sir got it. I can make your life very hard wench."

Daniel had been stood watching he liked this woman who ever she was nobody had stood up to John in years. Daniel said to John "you had enough strength carry those wenches to your bed so why cannot you carry just that one bag. "

"Yeah, well dear baby brother that was entertainment not coming home plus we have to my knowledge 30 servants so why would I do it myself ?"

John's face was livid at his brother's audacity to question his motives. '

"Marshall, saddle my horse I am going riding; I just need to change."

"Yes Sir, do you need helping Sir"

"By god man, no I can dress myself. Been doing it since I was five think I got the hang of it now lad. My horse Marshall "

"Sir sorry sir. "

John was about to walk to the stables after changing into his riding clothing when Sir Fredrick appeared'

"John come into my study, I want to talk to you"

The mystery of Lysham Manor by NanyWytch

John said to Daniel 'I expect it to do with whom will be master here should he die. Daniel my dear brother it will not be you. 'John smirks

Fredrick was waiting in the study as John Saunters in, '

"close the door and come sit here."

John was a bit puzzled at his father behaviour but did as he was bid.

Sir Fredrick slapped John across the face hard,

"How dare you charge all your expenses to me, I sent you money to pay your bills. Why were they not paid.? I did not mind paying for the axle but 30 guineas for a horse £30 dam guineas are you quite mad boy. £100 for a hotel room, enough drink keeps you insensible for a month. I do not think you have come round yet"

"Father I can explain"

"You do not have to the bill lists it all here in black and white. What happened to your allowance?"

"We err well, I lost it gambling at cards?" John broke off in a stammer,

"It seems to me you lose all the time, you ought to find something else to do instead like finding a wife."

"What are you thinking of you are 20 years old not 10, the upkeep of this estate costs a lot of money you have set me up onto the road to ruin do you not grasp people depend on me for a living."

John had not been spoken to like this by his father since he was 10, indeed he felt like that small boy right now. Fredrick continued'

" if you keep this up in two years you will have ruined this estate. We will have to sell the land and maybe the manor too to pay off your debts. You as master here what are you thinking boy. Get out tell your brother I want to see him."

John left the room worried; his father was really upset with him. John idealised his father to him it is how a master behaves towards others. he told his brother father wants you, mounted his horse and rode away fast. Daniel entered the study, '

"close the door sit here." Daniel was the better of the two boys he asked his father if he felt OK today. Fredrick said I am fine son, thank-you for asking.

"Daniel where did your allowance go?"

" Father you know what John is like he gambles, and drinks and he gambled his, then he took mine on that night we arrived in London. So, I wrote to you to warn you about the horse and axle. I had no idea he had charged our hotel to you. He has a problem father he drinks then he gambles, and he will not stop. What will become of me if he gambles the estate away once you are gone. "

"I have thought about this but need discuss things with my lawyer first. I know you have more sense than he does but you allow him to bully you. You need to start saying no what is mine is mine. You will need your money so you must learn to refuse your brother"

The mystery of Lysham Manor by NanyWytch

"It is harder than you think father, he is rough and arrogant and he well he just takes it without my consent I only find out afterwards that he has spent it.'

"Then I think I need find a way to stop him ruining the estate"

"May I go now father? "

"of course, did you meet Eileen"

"Oh yes father she stood up to John maybe she can help me."

"Yes, maybe she can she is just one year older than you are look how she deals with John. I hope you becomes friends she is rather special son. "

Daniel left the room, Eileen came in to ask if he was OK,

"'yes, I am fine, but it had to be said that boy will have me in ruins within a year if he does not alter his behaviours. Let me show you our costs just to run this place he opens a ledger it lists each person employed by the master their name wages and a place they signed the list stated '

Eileen sits down with him as he shows her the ledgers.

Henry butler £25 per year

Edward's valet £15 per year

Marshall Roche stable hand £16 per year

Game keeper Albert Finney £20 per year

The mystery of Lysham Manor by NanyWytch

Sarah Hunt Cook £25 per year

Leah upper house maid £15 per year

Mary lower house maid £11 per year

Scullery maid Mary £9 per year

Laundry maid £9 per year

Symons head gardener £25 per year

James's apprentice gardener £10 per year

Eileen's companion £15 per year

Farm labourers 8 of them £17 per year each plus cottage

John's valet £10 per year

Daniels's valet £10 per year

It does not include the casual labour we pay as needed.

That's just the staff it doesn't include Vets, lawyers, Drs and all the other things we buy in to keep standards up he was red and flustered he slumps into the chair mumbling that dam Dr charges me 5 shilling each dam visit most of the time he does nothing but he's been the family Dr years now since lizzie bare our sons. Plus, he's a close friend now I don't like owing any money so things are paid straight away.

Dam John 30 guineas for one dam horse when you can buy a decent one for £200 pull that carriage, he has no idea how much capital you need keep bye. Like the repairs for the west wing make it better are costing a pretty penny with Masons and joiners yet this we really do need this done it has not been touched since the fire if it has not done this year, it may never be rebuilt. It has been damaged since a fire burnt down the north wing nearly took the whole house if the servants had not got a line going with water, we would have lost the whole place. Do they know what caused the fire? They say a drunk servant dropped the candle but who knows this place has many spirits."

" Please do not get all worked up you know that you ought to be resting we do not want you going backwards I do not want lose you so soon. Over the past few months, you have come to be more like a father to me I know you are not and have no obligation at all to keep me here. But please Sir consider my feelings too and those of your lovely staff."

"I will be alright lass you worry far too much about others, now watch yourself around them you are not very worldly wise, and they are men"

" Sir you are worried for me, please do not be Sir I grew up in a small village with more boys than girls to play with I will manage fine."

"Good come on let us go sit in the drawing room rest up I will order our tea. Been a busy day so far let us hope tonight is calm shall we. Yes, she says walking with him to the drawing room." Daniel was sitting in their sketching he said "you were wonderful the way you dealt with my brother miss Eileen is it. Elle is simply fine. Your father told me the paintings are all yours you are a good artist"

" Well thank-you only father has seen them, I doubt they are worth much at all. "

Fredrick said

"now then maybe you are not thinking of this right Daniel maybe your paintings could bring you an extra income as they are rather good."

"I have many others father, I brought home a chest full, of paintings I did in Paris and Vienna of the sites there. Maybe you can look at them ask one of your friends if they might be worth selling."

"Of course, we can Daniel we will look at them later but for now I need rest and have afternoon tea are you joining us."

" No father I am going to ride into town get some supplies."
"Do you have any money? Awe Sir I was going to ask you could I have £5 please I assure you it is for art supplies."

" Here you are £5 do not you tell your brother. Of course, father thank you does you need any more snuff will be going in to buy cigars. Yes, please you know the brand do not you lad. Of course, father."

" Eileen, would you want to ride with me to town?"

Yes, If its ok with your father I enjoy riding"

" Yes, dear you go I need to rest now. "

"Thank you, Sir, "

When John came back with the horse it was beaten badly so badly it had gashes in its flank. Marshall Roche took the horse as John shouted him saying tend to the horse boy throwing the reins at him, stomping off again towards the house up to his room to change. The maid Mary was just placing towels on the bed, poor girl nearly died from shock as John came in yelling at her to get out. Slamming the door behind her

His mood had not changed by dinner which was earlier due to Sir Fredrick having a Drs visit. Once dinner was over John announced he was going into town. Marshall had tended to the horse as much as possible, but the poor thing had been run half to death it fell down onto the stable floor. Marshall came to the house to fetch the master, saying

"Sir your son John; rode the horse hard and beat it badly we need to contact the vet."

"Let me see says the master walking with Marshall to the stables, when he saw the condition of one of his prize's stallions, he was absolutely fuming at his son's audacity yet again. He said to his lawyer and to the Dr that he simply couldn't keep pretending his son was not just an absolute scoundrel. Today's behaviours made him think about the farm the house and the future of it all 40 people depended on this estate for a living He could not risk them all losing their work there was around 30 children who came at harvest as well as nearly all the village to gleam the fields after the harvesting. He always provided a good harvest supper with ale and cider for every worker.

He admitted its why he sent him off to London in the first place thinking a good school would alter the boy's character. His lawyer suggested he talk with him on the morrow about the estate as they needed get someone to run the farming side, now the master was aging. Daniel was simply not equipped to deal with his brother. He was far too artistic and musical he was so easy led that their father had seen it over and over how John bullied people into doing things his way.

The vet told the master that the horse would not heal from this beating it was too severe the horse would be so terribly scarred, and it would be affected in other ways. After looking at the deep cut on its leg the vet said it was better to shoot the poor thing than try to stitch its wounds. Sir Fredrick loved that stallion but agreed it ought to be put out of pain. So, he shot it himself.

John had gone to a tavern in town and he had drunk then gambled most of the night before passing out right there. However, a note John had signed was delivered by a man to Sir Fredrick.

The debt of £300 will be paid by my father Fredrick Gaunt

Signed John Gaunt

Fredrick read it and he swore as he asked the man where is this from? The tavern in town the big one called Cavendish, your son played cards last night and he lost badly. To Mr Pole. Your son told him it was all ok to give him credit as his father would pay.

Thank you, Sir will you ask Mr Pole, to visit me please so I can sort this out. He sent Marshall for his lawyer once Mr Baines senior was there Fredrick said

The mystery of Lysham Manor by NanyWytch

"he would need sell off some land in order clear this debt. After paying out for the debts the day before. Plus repairing the west wing," he was brushing back his hair from his face my son is going bankrupt me within a year."

He then listened to an idea the lawyers had that should he decide to give the manor to another it would be safer.

He agreed with his lawyers what he wanted done Mr Baines left with his instructions to sell one field of 4 acres to raise capital. It would fetch a good sum to release more funds into the estate as wages were due at end of month

John strolled into the manor still, worse the wear from drink, that he fell asleep on top of his bed. Fully clothed feet hanging off the edge he was oblivious a bill had already been sent from the tavern by the owner by messenger.

The following day Fredrick demanded his son joined him in his study, John walks in all smug and smiles at his father. "Fredrick nearly bursts a blood vessel raising his voice at John. He tells him the horse he ruined cost £500 then he said I had a bill come to my house this morning for yet another £300 gambling debts of yours.

I have had to sell off 4 acres of good farming land to cover this debt. Your current behaviour is showing your real character.

So, I have set up a trust fund for you to draw at aged 25 years old in the meantime you are leaving my house to go work to cover these expenses. I secured you a position at the lawyer's office as a clerk. You will reside above the office with the other clerks. Maybe having to earn your own money will teach you that life is simply not fair. Your bags are packed you are leaving at 4pm to start tomorrow. "

"But father you cannot do this to me, do you understand that people in the town know who I am they will talk father please what monies will I live on? "

"You will be given £20 for the first month then I like I said the lawyer's office will pay you weekly then it is up to you to manage your own monies like most people do"

" Father its degrading to make me work."

" No John its life, you owe me a dam fine horse plus the £900 you are going to work to pay it off, I have arranged with Mr Pole to grant you no further credit."

" Father you cannot just abandon me I am your son."

" John, you need to prove to me that you are responsible and can maintain your honour and status"

" You cannot just force me out of the house it is my home."

" Wrong boy it is my land, my house and it is about time you learnt how to treat other people now get out do not set foot on my land till you have paid off what you owe. If you are caught on the land the ground keeper has orders to shoot you"

" Father please I am sorry please."

Get out. Fredrick yelled his blood up; John was really shocked he never thought his father could be so tight fisted as this. He just did not see that he was wrong expecting his father pay for his errors of judgement. Now he was sent away yet again. It is that woman he thought getting into his head twisting him away from us. She is a conniving wench for sure, he was going do some research into her background find out whom she was what her intention might be around her father. He was getting old now. His health had not been good this last year. John thought about changes he would make as the master there he would be rid of her by god he would. He had toughened up his baby brother he was no contest for a girl like that one she would wrap him around her fingers in no time at all. Then from the carriage he sees where the clerks bed down it was a sort of shed building in the yard.

Daniel had heard it all from the next room he was having coffee with Eileen getting to know something about her. They both just looked at one another saying nothing till Eileen said "I hope your father is OK after getting upset like this twice."

"Yes, says Daniel I have not heard him so angry with John since we were boys. That horse was father's favourite. In one week, John has spent over £300 just at cards not to mention the brandy and loose women that cost one shilling a time. That is why we had two rooms not one I did not care sleep in same room as he has never shared since we slept in the nursery on top floor of the east wing. Have you seen the whole house yet? no not yet your father was not well enough, ok I will show you maybe tomorrow if you are not too busy.

Sending him away to work in a lawyer's office just in town. I hope he is not sending me away again."

Just as Daniel was called into the study. Straight after his brother

The mystery of Lysham Manor by NanyWytch

"Yes father"

" sit down Daniel I need to talk to you about your brother, he has been sent away to work to pay back the debts he owes to myself."

" Father are you sending me away to work too?"

" No son but I do want you to consider selling some of those paintings in the attic. You are a good painter I arranged for you to rent a gallery in the town not far from here we can hold an opening party next week let's get you set up with something you will enjoy doing"

"Thank you, father I love art,"

" I know son so whilst in town take a look there might be someone you might like in there."

His father had employed François from Eton collage whom he knew Daniel was friends with at school.

Daniel got along well with Eileen on their long walk. Daniel had shown her the gallery, she promised help him choose paintings display work out a price put on them.

" The manor and lands are all we have your brother has managed to spend all our capital; we have very little left in the bank son so your help will be appreciated very much so. I need employ an estate manager, I want you to help out too I need you to work alongside the estate manager who will be here tomorrow,"

" but I thought that would be John's job not mine. "

"Normally yes but he cannot be trusted right now to be responsible, so I am asking you."

"Of course, father I will try make you proud of me. "

"Daniel I am proud of you your art gives me pleasure."

" Thank you, father you have not said, that before"

" Well, I meant to now go enjoy painting."

Daniel leaves his father's study. Eileen knocks on the door to enquire as to his health. He sighs "deeply if only John could have changed his ways, then he would be working on the estate which would save me paying an estate manager £30 per year. Daniel is not really interested in the land. He will receive his monies on my death. John was to inherit as the eldest son, but he just is not ready for such responsibility. My decision is not what I had really envisaged for my old age. But it is the best. I can do for now. "

I understand shall we take a stroll as you have been so ill used today Sir, yes dear that would be nice as the sun sets.

They walk outside into the gardens; it is a lovely evening and Eileen simply wants him to realise that she is not going to leave him. The evening is a calm one as they gaze up at the nights sky.

Fredrick says you know dear; "I am so glad you did find my home that night. For your company is doing me very well. I never saw myself as enjoying a woman's company again, but you are a blessing. "

Eileen just nodded oh says Sir Fredrick "I have news about your aunt's property, she did leave a will everything belongs to you we can go take a look tomorrow if you like. "

"Yes, please really its mine. Yes, dear and there is more she left you £20,000 as well as the house. That means I am a fully independent woman, with my 2,000 a year from my family. so now I do not need paying to stay with you Sir,"

" yes it does but I hope this news does not mean you will be leaving me. "

"Oh, no sir I enjoy being with you I need to discuss this with you and Mr Baines of course as there will be legal papers to sign. Indeed, hence our appointment at 11am in town. "

"Will you be seeing John? "

"Heavens no child I want him to realise what he has actually done. So, you will leave him there? Eileen, I cannot tell you all my plans but for a while at least yes. "

The following day whilst in Haworth Sir Fredrick had only two things on his mind to help Eileen with her inheritance and to draft up papers for his will with Mr Blaine's senior.

At the office they started with Eileen inheritance first, the cottage was now hers to go see to do with whatever she wanted. The money she was going to invest in shares. Keeping only £1,000 in her account. The lawyer had said to her investing can be very dangerous, but it can also be profitable he had suggested shares in the oil company. Eileen was thrilled as it seemed a good investment to make. Eileen took the keys

The mystery of Lysham Manor by NanyWytch

to her cottage. Leaving Sir Fredrick to do his business in private.

As she walked down the main street, she bumped into John he grabbed her arm saying

"I know what you are up to, but I will not let you take my house and land so leave now."

She pushed him off her saying

"I don't need your house or land I have my own thank you plus I have my own income and not from your father either I agreed with him that I didn't need paying to be his friend."

John sneered at her said" then you can leave my family alone."

"Of course, says Eileen if it's what your father wants do you not see that your own behaviour has put you in this position with him nothing more, he was hoping that you had learnt from your long absence to be a real gentleman."

John sneered at her some more, saying" like I said you are not going to deprive me of anything. Not a wench like you out for what you think you can get well it will not be my land or my house lady"

"You talk as if your father is dead already Sir, I wish you goodbye "

John bumped into his father on the way up the hill "have you come fetch me home? "

"No, I intend to leave you here for a while actually let us go have lunch together just the two of us shall we son. Once seated at the black bull in a quiet corner near the blazing fire Sir Fredrick informed John that his will was now with Mr Blaine that due to circumstances beyond his control, he was leaving the estate to the care of another, but had set up monies for both his sons who were both free to live there." John stood up "you cannot be serious father; she is not even family plus she has money and a house. She does not need ours. Father it is just not right to dis inherit your sons. "

"John you are my son but until I can be assured you will be a good master on the land and care for other feelings the livelihood of all those whom work for us, I am leaving it as it is today."

"You mean if I stay here and make changes you want then you will alter it into my favour"

"That is correct John, I will let us say 3 months shall, "?

"Yes, father I will do it, you just see if I do not." They ate a good meal both laughing at a joke the landlord told them

"Let us hope for all our sakes you can keep your word, now I need to attend to Eileen and look at this house of hers"

"Have a good day father."

They parted company. Eileen had waited for Sir Fredrick at the house. She was standing in the sitting room deciding what to keep of her aunts' things. Now she could afford make it her own. It was hard for her as she had some lovely memories of spending holidays with her aunt in France and Spain.

The mystery of Lysham Manor by NanyWytch

Fredrick joins her he was surprised how big it was from the outside it looked tiny. The cottage was at the corner of Lodge Street where the Masons Lodge stood. You came in through the rather small door, into the sitting room. Off here were the stairs that were spiral metal ones, plus a small kitchen and dining room. Upstairs were 2 bedrooms of a good size plus a smaller room that her aunt had used as an office/workshop. Eileen went outside where the toilet was at the bottom of the garden. Fredrick asked what her thoughts were?

"Well, it would be a shame not to move into here, plus there is a lot to do with the sorting out what to keep. Would you be able to help me decide I was thinking If I stayed here but came see you each day? Or if you came to me as you are the one with the carriage. We could work together on this. "

"Of course, my dear you need to do this. Are you planning of spending the night here? "

"Oh no I do not think I want be alone just yet. It is far too soon for me I hope I might still, stay with you at the manor."

"Eileen of course you can I think of you as part of my family."

They returned to the manor for afternoon tea.

John hired a horse in Cornfield, he saddled the gelding pulling the frightened horse outside. Climbing into the saddle he dug is spurs into its flanks the horse bounded but John hit it to make it go forward. He rode up to the moors above themanor, where he could see the entire estate and the spire of Haworth Chapel where the family worshipped. His father's words went around in his head. I have decided to leave the estate in the care of another John struck a nearby Bush with his crop. I will kill her he said to himself sitting on the hillside looking down and what should be his. She will not keep the manor from me, yes, I will kill her. There was only the horse in earshot. He looked up then went back to eating the fresh grass. His anger abated he rode back into town. John started to think about his father what he had said to him, he thought of his attitude and mannerisms he talked to another lad from a rich house he too had been sent away by his father. John decided prove his father wrong he decided put his mind to business and do well here. His father had said 3 months that is not long at all to be away.

Meanwhile that night at the manor old Symons was in the garden wandering about tending the rose tree he had grown that he was going to name Eileen's tree. But Marshall Roche had been sent find him tell him supper was ready. Marshall found him lying on the floor. He was dead. They carried his body into the manor placing him on a bed in one of the rooms upstairs Daniel rode to fetch the Dr. Symons had told the boys stories of his youth when they were small helped them plant things for their mother. It was an hour before the Dr arrived, he had been with another patient. Did Symons ever speak of any ailment to you, no not to me he is has worked here since my father's days I think he began as a boy at 14 years old he must be at least 62 now. He was always a good man. Ok I will look at his body and determine cause of death for the paperwork then we must talk about his funeral. Does he have any family at all? No not as far as we know, nobody ever enquired about him. Dr said it was old age nothing untoward.

The mystery of Lysham Manor by NanyWytch

They arranged bury him in the plot on the manorial lands with other trusted servants.

At the service conducted by Reverend William Annaud it was Daniel, plus some servants who carried him after the funeral they returned to the manor for refreshments. It was obvious from the cold that winter would soon be throwing her icy blanket over Cornfield.

Sir Fredrick seemed to cheer up later into the day by spending time teaching Eileen play the harpsichord. She tried hard to learn it, but her mind and heart were wandering to her aunt's death. Months past bye quickly Eileen had nearly been there now a year, the cottage was hard to sort out but she had done a lot giving away what she didn't want to the poor around her. One day in March Fredrick asks Daniel and Eleanor if they would care to ride around the whole estate check-up how things are going, collect rents from the houses, out talk to his tenants about repairs.

. Well, if you feel your strong enough for this but we will go slowly. I am perfectly OK there is nothing wrong with me fresh air will not cure come on lass let us not waste the rest of the day.

They had Marshall fetch the horses but Fredrick, and Daniel picked up the saddles Fredrick said he would ride John's horse; she could ride his Daniel his own. I have no riding gear Sir, well if you look inside my wife's wardrobe you will find everything you need, we will go change to meet you outside. They mounted and set off. John had not set foot onto the land now in 2 months he had kept to his word and was applying himself to his work and studies of how the farming end could be improved cut the costs down He thought about the servants they did not have any valets he thought he ought to have his own as should Daniel it was the right thing for their status. He had been to see the working of now the corn exchange learnt the wheat, rye and barely was sold.

The mystery of Lysham Manor by NanyWytch

Chapter 5 the accident

They rode around the estate slowly then up into the hills above the land. They let the horses graze whilst sitting there chatting. Fredrick said to Daniel it would be nice have a painting of Symons, I have no idea how to replace him, but we must. They sat listening to the birds watching the horses munch the grass. How pleasant this it makes you forget your troubles. Eileen are you OK said Daniel, I watched you earlier you were very upset at the funeral. Yes, but I liked him a lot, it just reminded that I had missed my aunt's funeral so had not said goodbye. Did Symons mean a lot to your father? Well yes indeed they had known each other since they were children. Symons told me tales of what they got up to. Tell me father as a boy was a quiet naughty, he and Symons thought to help the gardener back then so when he went to lunch, they went to the greenhouse and they painted it. But they painted the windows too. Another time they were in the kitchen they saw the game keeper take in rabbits. They saw a pan on the stove and decided help, so they dropped a full rabbit into the pot. The cook Sarah did not know that it had not been skinned or gutted till it exploded guts and fur all over her nice clean kitchen. Another time he and Symons cut open a mattress to hide inside away from his father. Oh my god they were a bit of a pair. Yes, but these stories were how I grew up knowing my father was not so good himself as a child.

Fredrick got up off the log drinking from a hip flask said its time ride back, he had this glint in his eye tell you what I will race you both. Back at the stables Marshall was strolling up and down waiting for them to come back he had not noticed which saddle had gone onto which horse it worried him. When John had brought the other horse back damaged so badly it was shot. Marshall had cut John's girth strap in the hope he would fall from his horse. However, Fredrick was riding John's horse today on the way there they had slowly hacked their way up. Now they were riding fast down the hill. Fredrick was trailing behind them he felt uneasy like something was wrong. He felt the saddle slip on the horses back as the strap snapped but he was thrown off the horse. Fate had a way of its own the horse came down the hill without its rider. Eileen and Daniel turned back to find him. He was laying on the ground breathing slowly he was unconscious. She left Daniel with his father rode to fetch help. Eventually Sir Fredrick was carried home on a stretcher placed in his own bed. Marshall Roche had ridden for the Dr, but at the same time had gone to inform John of his father's fall. John had now been away nearly 10 weeks; he was looking forward to seeing his father talk about coming home. John panicked about his father if he died now, he wouldn't get the manor that girl would.

John rode like the wind back to the manor, Marshall was left to walk. John arrived as the Dr was just arriving himself. Good day John I had warned your father to take better care of his health, but what on earth has happened today. It was a riding accident I believe I was not there. Just Daniel and Eileen. Heading upstairs to Fredrick's room the Dr asked the family wait outside.

Marshall Roche went to see Eileen in the study excuse me ma'am could I speak with you please? It is about the accident ma'am it is my job check over all the saddles and straps. Well, everyone hates Master John with a vengeance. It was me ma'am I am responsible for this. If I had noticed which saddles were picked up of the rail, I would have not let them uses master John's saddle. What has done is done now we will not speak about this again we cannot let master John find out or it will be your job. I will Let you all know how he his later. The Dr left the room saying he will return later with another Dr. Eileen went to sit with him. John and Daniel were asking questions about their father they were answered with yes, I am worried he has not woken up yet so he might have a head injury. Eileen left to have tea; on her return she saw him sitting up propped against pillows Leah was with him. She left as Eileen returned. Fredrick said to her holding her hand I need to speak to my lawyer; again, will you send Marshall to fetch him. Do not say anything about it are both my sons here as I think I heard John's voice out there. Yes, Sir they are both here you have been unconscious for over four hours.

Eileen in town the other day I made plans for the manor I want it to live on the way it is. But I know John will squander it. I left instructions it was to go to you. Will you accept it as I have trust in you to do the right thing. But Sir your sons ought to come way before me do not they have legal claim to it even if it is in your will. Eileen listens to me if they can prove I was not making the right choices about things because. I had gone mad, otherwise no they cannot contest the will.

The Drs came back happy to see him sitting up awake, they examined him again found he had hurt his head when he fell. They insisted that he rest he was forbidden from getting out of bed. Over the next few days, he seemed to get weaker and slept a lot. Eileen sat with him whilst the brothers argued downstairs when John told Daniel about father leaving the estate to her. Sir Fredrick got stronger his health returned to him he started to shut himself away in the study with the new estate manager. John wanted to prove to his father he had changed his ways, so he wrote to him about a machine that could plough a field in half the time it normally took. He wanted his father come see this machine. He met with him they visited a neighbouring estate to see the machine in action in a day 3 fields had been ploughed and seeded. Sir Fredrick decided it was worth buying one to increase production. They could plough up another field leave those fallow that had been used the year before. John and his father were getting on well as johns' interest in the farming side of the estate improved things between them. At lunch that day John asked if he might come home but be involved in running the estate with his father. Sir Fredrick wanted his son to come work alongside him teaches him how the estate ran. Costs involved; John was happy to oblige his father they grew close again. That Christmas John had requested if they might hold a ball like mother used to. Fredrick thought it was a good idea as then John might find a woman he liked enough to marry. Fredrick knew his other son would never marry as his sexual inclinations ran the other way.

They held a ball on 21st December it was the first time the new ballroom had been used as 20 guests were to stay over whom had brought extra servants with them the kitchen was a bit crowded for Sarah, she had catered all the food for the ball in three days of hard baking and cooking, ham, pheasant, duck, she had made Pattie pickles pies and cakes.

The mystery of Lysham Manor by NanyWytch

Feeding near on 60 people was a task and a half. But it was done. Thankfully. Fredrick surprised the staff by bringing a dozen bottle of champagne and a barrel of ale to them. Saying this is your party too enjoy.

The ball where a wonderful night Eileen had not danced like this before so many men being attentive to her. Her dance card filled up so fast one man in particular had four dances talked to her a lot she liked him till Daniel told her waster drunk used women's monies then he left them.

 The next day she had morning tea with some of the women one of them was heard to say she thought Eileen too lower class for such a house that she was possibly the poor relative they felt sorry for. The same woman told another she thought Eileen's hair resembled a bird's nest, that her skin was extremely poor. Her hands were rough like she belonged outside. Eileen held her tongue till she heard another story the same female had spread about that she was Johns' whore not at all a lady of consequence. At this Eileen sat down next to Lucy Wainwright and said to her Lucy, I heard you think I am a whore, and that my hair resembles a bird's nest. In which case I think your own skin sallow, your dress very poorly put together, but most of all I have heard that John had you in your father's barn not two weeks ago. Lucy stood up brushed down her dress and said I will not remain here to be insulted I am leaving she stomped off. The other ladies said to Eileen is it true she has been with John in the barn. Oh yes says Eileen plus she was the one chasing him not the other way round.

Christmas came and went as a simple affair, just family and Eileen. Johns interest in business matters grew he attended the corn exchange with his father to see how well their wheat, barley & rye sold. Fredrick was very happy John was thinking more about the estate than gambling. He told John he would have the will altered in his favour. At the next visit to the lawyer's office a couple of weeks hence. John was so happy he danced about the grounds singing to himself, he was in such a good mood he hugged the maids kissed them on the cheeks said thank you which was simply never done by him they were shocked at his turn about. The talk downstairs was he had gone mad.

A week later just 2 days before the lawyer's appointment Fredrick was feeling fitter than he had been in years wanted go for a ride with Eileen about the estate. As they were riding about the estate slowly. Something startled the horse it reared up throwing Fredrick to the ground he fell hard and fast without any chance of remaining on the distressed horse which bolted off across the field. Eileen was on the ground with Sir Fredrick, talking to him. Workers came over from the farm she sent one to fetch the Rd. Then asked the men carry him to the house. They placed him down on the sofa in the drawing room. It was only minutes before John and Daniel were there whom insisted, they took their father to his room upstairs. Fredrick had not spoken at all just moaned in pain. The Dr came to tell them that their father had broken a few ribs fractured an arm and hit his head badly this time. That all they could do was wait to see if the bang to his head would heal. John was very attentive to his father as was Daniel during this time. Eileen, sat with him holding his hand. Staff called in with tea and broth to keep his strength up. But Fredrick never regained consciousness

Sir Fredrick died in his sleep on the 9th August 1858. Eileen found him she had just placed the tray down with his breakfast on it. But Fredrick was cold his eyes closed. He looked so peaceful laying there. She burst into tears holding his hand when Leah came in to light the fire. Is the master alright miss? No Leah he has gone from us. Daniel was the first to enter after Leah had passed on the message that he was dead. He covered his father's face with the bed sheet after kissing his head. Then left to make sure the Dr was called back in. As well as the Reverend. The funeral was just a few days later his body was interned in the family crypt.

Weeks pass by the servants tried to carry on as normal but the mumbling below stairs were that it depends very much who is Master here now. As if some or all may wish to leave. They decided after the will they would stay if Miss Eileen was in charge but if it were Master john, they might be best at the mill.

Chapter 6 I bequeath

The lawyer stated his business on arrival at Lysham Manor, he offered his condolences on their sad loss of a wonderful father friend and landowner. He said that the will was lodged in his care some time ago. Everyone was seated in the library even the staff.

The lawyer read

This is the last will and testament of myself Frederick John Gaunt being of sound mind and body at the time of writing. I have decided to leave all my estate to miss Eileen Mason Perry who was my companion in my last months of my life. To my sons John who spent most of his adult life trying ruin me and the estate trying to bankrupt me I have set up monies for you to live this will be yours at age 25 years. Daniel will receive the same amount and his gallery You are permitted live in the manor and help run the estate, but title and deeds are Eileen's. To Marshall Roach I leave £200 To my beloved Sarah I leave £400 to Leah £200 to Mary £200 for the labours on the estate they are to have the cottages in perpetuity plus their incomes increased to £20 per year I leave all my wife's clothes and jewellery to Miss Eileen Mason Perry,

Fredrick John Gaunt

You are a lyre roared John he was not serious he told me he was going change it. Leave it all to me. John snatches the paper from the hands of Mr Blaine's senior. Who was astounded at the boy's behaviour and manner? Never in all his years as a lawyer had he been called a liar.

Daniel sat quiet as a mouse, but John turned all his malice towards Eileen it is all your fault this you coddled my father in these last month's whilst you made him hate me. You scheming little bitch. Eileen kept her composure and replied now that the will has been read John if you cannot accept your father's choice then I suggest you find somewhere else to reside. Is your bloody insane wench this is my home I will not be turned out of it by anyone? Then John you and your brother will work for me by keeping things running smoothly on the estate but ever mind that I am now mistress here all decisions are mine. John nearly broke a blood vessel I am a gentleman I do not work this is mine he yelled shaking Eileen. Why do we employ servants they do the work not me? Eileen stood up to John that was before you tried ruin your father with your debts, he threw you out himself less than a 3 months ago. Got you a job in Mr Baines office I do believe well I will employ your skills here instead you can start in the morning. To hell with you bitch. He storms out of the house. Sir she said to the lawyer will you write up a document for me to state that John and Daniel are permitted remain on the estate sharing the house as long as they work to maintain it. Of course, Eileen it will be ready to sign tomorrow by the boys and yourself I also need to know about money in the bank and how we access this to pay our staff.

Of course, Fredrick left that in my care all you need do is tell me what you need miss it will be brought here to you. Thank you, Sir, for all you have done. Good day ma'am. John came back into the house can she do this to us by law we are blood relatives she is nothing. Not even our class. Yes, the will is legal and if you do not sign the conditions paper then she can ask you to vacate the manor. Unless of course the young lady marries you or your brother then the property becomes her husbands he becomes master here that is the law Sir.

John stands there staring at Eileen the only woman who had the audacity to argue with him in front of the staff. He felt so angry that she now controlled the manor and the land as well as his father's money. Daniel had not spoken a word all this time John turns on him has it sunk into your mind my little brother.

Why should I care I was never the eldest son nor the pampered son? You want the manor but to get it you now need bend the knee to a wench. Frankly, I very much doubt she even likes you. John walked into the study slammed the door shut, he started to drink, later he was found lying in his own sick still holding the empty bottle of whiskey.

They managed get him upstairs into his bed, they undressed him then Daniel left the room suddenly John sprang to life grabbing Eileen pulling her towards him he dragged her to him kissing her full on the mouth holding onto her hair she could not struggle much. He yanked her arm dragged her over to the bed roughly pushed her down holding one arm behind her, his elbow in the middle of her back he was a big man his strength far outweighed any struggling Eileen did, but she wriggled out of it stood up, he grabs her again this time he put a knife to her throat Eileen's tried to be coy, give that to me you fool, you could cut yourself with it. He pressed it into her neck drawing blood Oh look he said the creature bleeds pity it is not blue.

Now you are going to give me what I want. You are going to Marry me we are going to have the manor together. He smirks at her she screams at him No it is not happening I promised your father I would not allow you to bully me into submission, He pushed her into the bed holding her down dragged up her dress then he mounted her backwards like a horse. Forcing himself into her awaiting quim. He was very rough holding onto her hair as he ramped against her small body she was screaming in pain, after he had finished, he stood up smiling at her Now wench you are mine any issue from this is mine. But you can be sure wench I will ensure you will agree to my terms He laughs; Eileen was terrified there was no mercy in this man's eyes at all. She became the unwilling participant in his sexual games. She knew it was no good trying to fight him, so she did not fight at all. A Virgin no more Eileen now you are mine. I am sure that the law would believe a gentleman rather than a street girl. The next morning

Eileen confronts John at breakfast rape will not get me to marry you sir you are a brigand. Do sit down woman its far too early to have words with my intended. If you are carrying my child, you will indeed need a husband, or your reputation will be rubbish amongst society you are just a mere woman nothing more sweet tasting Eileen. She sat to eat breakfast this was pointless. Daniel joined them the conversation was somewhat stilted. Eileen said they needed meet with the estate manager today to know what needed attending too. John said first I intend have my morning ride then I am going to get very drunk. Eileen reminded John that the lawyer would be here soon with the papers to sign. Indeed, he said sign it yourself then wench I am busy today. John went riding up into the Moor above the estate he let the horse eat the grass whilst he sat on the grass drinking from the flask in his pocket. He was going have to bide his time, he decided he liked the idea of sex with this bitch it was good, she fought hard he liked this idea he decided he was going to enjoy this game if she were pregnant then she might concede to save her reputation. John made sure he grabbed Eileen in the barn or on the stairs anywhere he could pull her away so he could force himself on her she suffered a lot from his rough sexual advances she was bruised so badly it bled on her inner thighs. Eileen grew fatter with child. A child she detested more than John as it was a product of his rapes. The time came near for the birth, in the agonies of Labour she cursed John. A drunken good for nothing spineless bastard. He had learnt during her pregnancy that she was even more determined to stand up for herself she dug her heels in about every suggestion he made regarding the estate management. Yet she knew nothing of running a place as big as Lysham manor. This irritated John very much as he now knew all about running the estate. He had learnt about business and investments, the corn exchange and all he needed to know about the law. John became a formidable man he had learnt a lot whilst away from the manor but anytime something went wrong, he threw a temper fit at people often becoming violent.

Chapter 7 Decent

An idea was brewing in johns mind, but it needed incredibly careful planning he would take his time there were important things to consider unless they were married, he would not gain what he wanted there had to be a wedding. But how could he get her to marry him? He thought long and hard decided he would need resort to more serious methods. He went to see the priest at the church to talk to him saying I have made a grave error and a girl of my house is now with child which is mine. I need to marry this girl to save her reputation. can it be done quickly or is it against your church policy not to marry pregnant girls is it not me making restitution for the wrong I did to her. The Priest had known John since being a boy, they had spent time together when he was in the choir before he went off to school. He considered his reply.

John, have you asked the woman concerned for her consent spoke to her family? NO father she has no family left I wanted to ask your consent first as she is important to me. So, John answer me truthfully, I heard rumours that you intend to marry Eileen. Well yes Sir I do you love this woman john of course I do at first it was all pure like a sister but now it burns inside me so hot I think I need to be with her she is vibrant and tough and wild like me. I will give you my blessing, but you need her consent to do this or it will not be legal. Yes, Sir thank you Sir have a good day john left walking into the Black bull where he met his friends, they got rather drunk. He staggered back to the estate early morning fell asleep outside on the lawn. He decided he needed to make her love him by being nice to her and giving her anything she wanted so she would see he was really kind now a bastard.

It was only an idea forming in his head if he killed her how could he do it plus what to do with the body John turned it around inside his head till it was all he could think of one day maybe a week later drunk as per usual, John said to himself the cellar yes, the cellar its only used for wine and locked the owner having the key. Daniel would never agree to murder he liked her. Maybe if he were drunk, he could make him help. John stole the key off her belt whilst she was sleeping. He had a copy made in town then replaced the master key. There were builders fixing up the west wing, maybe he could find a place there as it was hardly used right now so many deserted parts of the manor. He thought only about getting rid of her anyway he could. She was not having what was rightfully his by birth. Trouble was the walls were built so very thick over 6ft wide in places. The manor was very old building materials had changed since his grandfather had the place built. He watched the builders constructing a wall in the west wing one day seeing how a cavity is left in the middle. His mind turned over he smiled to himself he needed get his brother on his side first. It had to be perfect. So, he bided his time.

Eileen gave birth to a healthy little girl, but she refused to tend it or touch it, to her this was the product of John's rape. John had employed a wet nurse Eileen refused visit the nursery instead spending time at the farm getting to know more about the way things were done. How the butter and cheese were made. She got to know all the staff even the farm hands and their families who would starve come winter without gleaming the fields for left over wheat, rye, and barley that was grown.

The mystery of Lysham Manor by NanyWytch

Not to mention the vegetables they but the staples were the grains. Each had a piece of land grow veg in outside their cottage the wives did this work, as well as tend the family. There was talk of a cotton mill coming to Cornfield, many of the women were talking about getting work there but it was a 5-mile walk to town. If they did, they would be getting up at 3am to get to work by 6am they would do a 12-hour shift then have walk home and tend to food the house laundry the children it looked like it was just a dream for one shilling per day. The poster in the village said they were taking on children as young as 8 years old, but they would earn only 6 pence per day. Maggie had 4 lads who were old enough go to the mill. The terms were difficult as the mill said it would accommodate children feed and clothe them till, they reached 18 as interred workers most knew nothing about what it meant one of the men approached Eileen saying if we send our boys to the mill what does it mean

Eileen said it meant that the boys would belong to the master of the mill they would own them till they were 18 they would be able see you only on Sundays. He said I do not know if it is better, they were working or better they went to the village school. Eileen said they would always be offered work here. But farming was changing too machines were able do a man's job, so he needed look to the future.

It worried her if they lost the farm workers where would they get more. Like he said things were changing it was now 1858 The child was growing up fast, but Eileen still refused see her, so the poor child was cared for by her nurse.

The mystery of Lysham Manor by NanyWytch

John decided to get Eileen alone in the stables late at night when Marshall would be with the other staff in the kitchens relaxing. So outside would be quiet. That evening Eileen was walking outside in the cool night air. John forces her into the stables. Pressing his whole body against hers moving one hand up her thighs he pushes his fingers into her. She moves but cannot move out of his way. Being held close by him did feel nice as he was a very handsome man. He was kissing her neck very gently she stopped struggling started kiss him back. He managed have sex with her in the hay this time it was consensual. They rolled about in the hay talking softly with each other. Eileen enjoyed the kisses and his smell; she had fancied him for months. She argued with him daily about things but the two got along well really. John simply adapted his plans seriously putting thought into each move he made.

In secret they each shared thing only the intimate people share. One night just before the child's first birthday John asked Eileen to marry him. She consented. A month later they were married in Haworth Church. They took two weeks away visiting her property in Devon. They decided to sell it, they had rented out the cottage as well. This money was kept at the house some £1,000 for the house in Devon and rent for cottage was 5 shillings a month.

Eileen was very happy for a few months as John was cutting back on drink. He had access to her monies now and to all the monies of the estate. He wanted hold a shoot for some 15 men the following weekend. Eileen objected he hit her in their rooms. Eileen did not come down that day nor for a few days. John wanted play these rough games for sex. He liked to beat her with a riding crop before having sex it enhanced it for him.

The mystery of Lysham Manor by NanyWytch

After all John was used to going with whores where anything was ok. He had never been with a more refined person. But as his wife she had no recourse. Daniel saw his brother strike Eileen, he stopped him taking john's arm. To which John responded by punching his brother. Eileen went to tend Daniel, John dragged her away locking her in her rooms.

The shoot went well, but John got very drunk played cards lost £400 that night. Eileen was livid with him saw her lawyer put an order in place to protect her own monies from being squandered. Much to Johns' anger that night he really beat Eileen breaking her arm and some ribs. When Leah saw her, she had Marshall fetch the Dr. He came to Eileen seeing her in private asking her to say what had happened. She claimed to have fallen from her horse. Drs Stroud knew it was a lie. John was drinking heavily his moods were very bad he yelled at the staff. When sober the next day he did not recall how he had behaved.

Eileen had now prevented him from taking monies without her signature. She gave the Dr a handwritten letter sealed it said give this to the Lawyer, John walked out of here alone. He still held nightly card games saying his wife would pay the damages. One night in a drunken state he got poor Sarah the scullery maid against a wall he forced himself on her. The poor girl could not tell anyone for fear of losing her place. John kept pulling the girl towards him in the churning room. She started like his company he promised he would see her settled in the cottage in town. She believed him, but when she fell pregnant, he sent her packing with just one month's wages saying get off this land and do not come back. Poor Sarah had nothing prove the child was johns. She had nothing prove his promises either. She killed herself in a cellar room in gangers croft the poorest housing in Haworth. John had spoken to Baines who had told him he wouldn't get the manor till his wife died as conditions were in place to protect the manor.

When Eileen's child was 18 months old, they held a small party at the manor just the three of them were to be at the dinner. John had not been idle he had been preparing his plan. They ate roast beef with all the trimmings drank port wine and brandy but on the second glass John added a sleeping draft to it before handing it to Eileen. It was not long before it started to work. She felt so tired she could not explain it on her third drugged glass she fell asleep on the couch. Daniel was drunk near enough insensible. John was strangely sober. He had planned every detail of this for over 2 years.

Daniel helps me carry her, so Daniel helped his brother carry Eileen John why are we going this way? Because my dear brother we are getting rid of her. What he slurred are we doing? It does not matter little brother it is just a bad dream. I can manage now you go to bed. Yes, ok are you sure! Of course, I am he put Eileen over his shoulder, she moaned a bit but was still sound asleep. Daniel mumbled why will we be without a home if I do not help you. Daniel I will explain in the morning at breakfast go to bed before you collapse too. Daniel came back to John; I will help you I can help. Ok then you take her legs they carried her to the cellar where John had prepared a place for Eileen. John placed her in the cavity he had dug out still unconscious. Daniel fell down drunk on the cellar floor. John began bricking up the wall with Eileen inside it. Indeed, this dug out space would be the grave for Eileen Mason Perry. Once he had finished, he grabbed Daniel dragged him up to his bedroom. Going back to the cellar to fetch a few bottles of brandy and port wine upstairs. He locked the door to the wine cellar pocketing the key.

The mystery of Lysham Manor by NanyWytch

Chapter 8 the curse

Eileen slept on so totally unaware of what had occurred as yet the sun rose of the next morning at 4am outside John had not yet slept indeed he needed to know that the plaster he had put over the bricks had set and was drying he estimated she would not wake for another 12 hours or more.

So, he went down the cellar to check his work the house was still quiet the staff did not rise till 7am to begin lighting fires and cleaning up. The family did not eat till 8am normally sometimes it had been 9am. John examined his work it was setting nicely 2 layers of cemented bricks covered with 4 inches of thick quick setting plaster.

He was content so locked it up again to go onto his next part of his plan. He had decided it was best that the child was gone as well. He woke Sarah up told her that he wanted her to go home to her cottage in the village taking the child. That he would pay her to take care of the child and visit her whilst she was still very small. He said she ought to bring her up as her mother he would pay for her to go away to school when she was 7 years old. But Sarah was to take care of her. He had taken the child from the nursery and then he drove the carriage to cornfield with Sarah and the baby aboard.

He returned to the manor knowing the staff would be waking up soon, he replaced the horses and trap into the stables knowing Marshall slept above here. He was used to hearing the odd neigh from a horse at night. Hours passed by before the staff were awake, they found a note from Sarah saying she had another position and was leaving as she hated goodbyes.

The mystery of Lysham Manor by NanyWytch

The nurse woke to find no child and came down to see if a maid had her when they could not find her, they worried something terrible had happened to it. John was in the drawing room reading the papers. When Mary came to light the fires, Master John the baby is missing. What do not be silly she cannot even walk. Maybe Eileen has her after all she is the mother, but Sir she has made no attempt even see her in the six months since her birth. Well maybe she just needed time before accepting her. I suppose you might be right he told the nurse check the nursery see if anything is missing. Then knock to wake Eileen see if the child is with her.

Leah came to see Master John Sir Sarah is gone too; she loved that child. The nurse came back if you please Sir the babies clothing and things are all gone even her bedding is gone. Have you told Eileen no Sir as we do not think she would care either way? Leah went to Eileen's rooms, to discover the bed not slept in and the clothing all gone along with things from the dresser. Sir she is not here all her things have gone. Then I expect Eileen and Sarah have the child. Which means we no longer need the nurse send her to me.

The nurse comes to see Master John knowing she was going be dismissed she kept saying sorry Sir. John hands her a letter of recommendation gives her a month's salary. The nurse leaves the estate in tears.

Leah informs John that they need another cook, that she can do it today, but she has other work too. Do not worry Leah we will get one. I will go myself to put an advert in the local paper and one in the post office. Thank you, Sir, does this mean Sir that you are the Master now. I have no idea, yet I need speak to the lawyer today. Now my wife has left me stolen my child away, he acted all upset so Leah comforted him saying maybe she would come back John Mumbled under his breathe no it is over now.

By the time Eileen began to wake discovering she was inside the wall in a very confined space she could not stand, only kneel. Realising she had been buried here alive. She let out a piercing scream, but it was not heard anywhere in the house.

She banged on the walls scratching at them with her fingers she was screaming and screaming in her exhausting efforts to try scratch the cement she broke nails. Her fingers were bleeding, but she still scratched and screamed then falling back she went quiet trying to think of how she could get out. She knew in her heart this was johns doing only he would be so cruel. She remembered last night feeling drunk and tired, but she had no memory of anything more than being in the drawing room. She thought of poor sweet weak Daniel had he been forced to comply with his brother. She scratched into the cement

I who lie uneasy here

Will haunt forever year by year

Until this place in ruins lie

For only then will the evil die.

She wrote her name as Eileen

The mystery of Lysham Manor by NanyWytch

The air was running out she was feeling very tired, weak her hands were bleeding the writing was in her own blood. As she sank into death.

John had drunk several glasses of port wine Daniel was pacing the floor his head pounding for god's sake sit down will you Daniel says how can you just sit there drinking. Give me the key I will break it down get her out. No Daniel she is not our blood line father was wrong for god's sake man the girl came off the street 3 months before our father was so besotted, he signed it to her do not you see it is our home always will be. Daniel said all I know is that when I was pissed as a fart you convinced me to help carry her. I do not recall actually burying her I must have gone out cold, so I did not do anything just you. No brother you helped me before you passed out. I did not want to harm her she was nice to me. What do you want me to say I am glad you killed a young girl buried her in the dam cellar? John, we have to get her out Daniel he says holding his brother by the shoulder, if we do that, she will have us both hung. Do you want to be hung? No, I will say I did not do anything. Daniel the staff all know what went on here between us. Do not you realise that they hear conversations and listen to things watch us. Daniel starting downing brandy after brandy I cannot condone this, John; I cannot live with this then you need to grow some balls and simply keep your mouth buttoned or you might end up in a wall too. Daniel was frightened of his brother always had been, so he drank more brandy trying to forget what he knew. Daniel had never been a heavy drinker, but it helped block out the idea he could be hung for holding her legs. Helping take her the cellar. It scared him a lot.

The mystery of Lysham Manor by NanyWytch

Put it out of your mind go paint something, if you mention this again, I will beat you insensible. However, Daniel do not let it drive you mad just forget it happened like dreams. You will regret this John maybe, but I will not fret about now it has done. If you cannot reside here go live somewhere else, how can I without substantial funds.

John sat fondling the key turning it round in his hand, I am putting this where prying eyes cannot find it. I do not need a key get into the cellar John if I did Henry has one. Does he it is a no this is his key. I will break the door down with the axe, in the cellar little brother. If you do anything we will be hung as murders.

The mystery of Lysham Manor by NanyWytch

Chapter 9 Legacy

Sarah's yearly allowance was 12 Guinea's lot of money for a mere cook to have, John bought her a new larger house with a garden a bit away from the centre of the village. He visited his daughter whilst she was still young, at 7 years old she was sent away to boarding school. The story was that Eileen had left to see a distant relative giving the child to the cook Sarah as she did not trust the men with it alone. It was accepted by everyone as extremely plausible. Eileen was forgotten Symons forgotten Marshall Roche was suddenly dismissed by John. Eleanor Hunt was brought up thinking Sarah was her mother as she grew up with her own children. She was told nothing about the manor at 7 years old she attended boarding school at the same time John made it possible for Sarah's two boys go a good school to.

John & Daniel lived it up giving ladies nights with several whores. dance parties with drunken card games. The manor started to fall into disrepair, the farm suffered the most as John sold off acre after acre to pay off gambling debts from his heavy losses.

Half the staff were let go, another few resigned. So, he hired new They stayed only a short time when they thought they might never be paid.

John was walking about the manor grounds one summers day a year after Eileen's death around at the South Wing he heard banging he saw a window in that wing the shutters banging in the wind. Yet it was only a breeze that day. John carried on walking but as he glanced up to the window of Eileen's room, he could swear she was standing there gazing out at him. His logical mind cast the thought away. That it was evening shadows playing tricks on him. He decided to go upstairs to close the window. The only servants inside the manor now were Mary and Leah who took care of everything the laundry was sent out.

They bought groceries in now instead of it coming from the farm all that was grown now was wheat and rye. There was no livestock except a few chickens. The horses had been sold off excepting 3 of them 2 to pull the carriage and john's horse. Daniel did not care to ride these days he shut himself off in the west wing painting during the day drinking at night. John had not replaced Symons and he got rid of the under gardener as he did not like his tone of address.

The gardens were now becoming unkempt, the external house looked decayed and neglected the ivy had spread covering a few windows at the front it climbed into the gutters causing rain to flood down a wall. The roof leaked into the attic; servants' rooms began locked up forgotten about. Leah and Mary could only tend to one wing of the house the west wing which had been extended with a ballroom and games room. Sir Fredrick turned in his grave if he could see his beloved manor.

That weekend John gambled the horses and carriage on one turn of a card. Most of the money had gone now. So, John sold off the last fields the farm now gone the men laid off. They were meant to still have their cottages as Fredrick had wished in his will but John had other ideas, he would rent them out so if they had no work they had to get out. Some of the men were extremely angry at John arguing the cottage were legally theirs

John said get off my land right now or I will dam well shoot you he stood over them whilst they emptied their things, they left all of them John said good riddance he was drunk of course.

The stables were empty as he then lost his own horse at another card game. Between them with two years they had destroyed what was once a thriving estate with magnificent gardens and a thriving farm.

John was far too fond of drinking to care a once well stocked wine cellar was almost empty, when Sir Fredrick was alive the apples were sent away to make cider, the pears for wine. Wine was bought in London in large orders that were delivered by cart. Now there was little, but no special wines left very few cases of decent whiskey or brandy. Yet he did not care about anything except self-gratification. Daniel the weaker man his mind tangled in thoughts good and bad remembers Eileen's smile her shine of her hair that glistened in the afternoon sun. Her eyes that were a bright blue, her manner and the compliments on his painting. Daniel had actually made a good income from his art. He had bought a gallery in Cornfield from his trust fund. He was doing quite well. Yet suffered these terrible night terrors. Daniel had painted a full-size portrait of Eileen just before her death he hung it near the window of her room, so light would catch her eyes. He would say he had seen her walking the gardens early mornings or seen her wandering the dark corridors of the hall. Every night he would scream go away it was not me who did you harm, go away leave me be please. He would wake up wet from sweat, drenched his heart racing. He walked the rooms for the rest of the night or shut himself off in his attic studio for days at a time.

John arrived at Eileen's room mid-afternoon, he had been drinking and was rather tired. He walked into the room then he stood back as he swore, she was there, seconds later he realised it was the painting he had seen being done 2 years before he was angry so smashed it, he didn't want to see her face, her eyes smiling at him, that red hair tumbling off her shoulders. That perfect shaped female embodiment. In his own way he decided he did love her if his father had given the property to him maybe things might have been good for him the sun was casting shadows into the room that had been ignored since her death. Although it was clean of dust other areas were neglected, they seemed cold and empty. Yet he could smell her scent in that room, feel her essence. It was now nearly 3 years since her death.

John leant out the window it was the rounded one he could not quiet reach the catch, so stood up to look if there was a poker or something help grab that catch. Pull the window shut. Close those wooden shutters that banged in the wind. He used a coat hanger, as he leaned out something tickled his neck and that smell of her drifted past his nose, he glanced up still leaning out that window saw Eileen standing near him as if she were alive in that blue chiffon evening gown, she wore that night with that string of pearls he had given her for Christmas when his father was alive. Her hair was cascading over her right shoulder, her eyes shone but her facial features look more terrifying than anything he had ever seen her mouth wide open as if in a scream her eyes were like big black holes her teeth looked jiggered but her hair shone in its glory it was longer more beautiful something about her enticed him to remain still keep looking.

. Her fingers all bony Spidery he was transfixed by what he saw he had stood up staring at her as she came closer that dress making a sweeping noise over the wooden floor. He heard her voice sprinkled on the evening breeze. His mind was trying to grasp what he was actually seeing, but he had drunk during the afternoon he was tired. So, he told himself this was not real at all how could it be she was behind that wall in the cellar hidden behind a shelving of fine wines.

No, it was not her maybe a servant it looked two reals to be a ghost. She was right in front of him the words came from her wide-open skeletal features

Now she was right in his face her fingers crawled up his flesh making him scream on the inside. She reached his neck then she grabbed him and pushed him. His balance being compromised by the fact he was leaning backwards away from her, the expression on her face was contorted hate. He fell two stories to the ground below his head smashing on the ground like that of an egg dropped into a pan. Daniel heard the scream as he was coming up the drive from town. He ran to his brother, laid over him John oh no John do not leave me please stay with me. His eyes were wild with terror his mouth open as if in a scream. He moaned Eileen she is. Then he was dead. Daniel looked up at the windows to see Eileen's red hair blowing out the window, that open mouth wearing a smile, Daniel cried over his brothers' body for a long time. Leah had seen the fall as she was picking flowers for in the house. She went for the Dr, who declared John dead on October 20th 1862 aged just 22 year the shock of his brother's demise sent Daniel into a mental breakdown where he painted a series of very dark pictures mostly containing Eileen as he saw her in his dreams. As time passed, he spent most of his time in the study. More of the land was sold off. The outside building all began to go into ruin. He claimed she haunted him at night, that in the day he saw her in the library, or drawing room laughing on the sofas. He claimed she taunted him, laughing at his weakness. He claimed at night she would be in his room staring at him, her mouth wide opens her spidery fingers touching him. He would scream and cry. Leah was near on 40 years old now she was a servant there when he was born, back then she was only 20-year-old, she knew that blonde curly head boy with the mischievous smile whom at 7 went away to school crying holding a bear he called Brian. She knew the teenager whom still with that hair that he refused could be cut. Those chubby cheeks and plumper body than his brother. She remembered him sneaking into the kitchen at night for hot chocolate raiding pantry for cheese and bread. She would walk him back to bed give him a motherly hug. In fact, she was the only one who was close to him, the only female he trusted. Daniel told Leah it was her you know she is back. She pushed him I saw her face it was awful. Leah would lay next to him till he went back to sleep, she and Mary had moved into rooms on this floor now. As time passed Leah left claiming she could not stay because things happened there without explanation. Such as rooms catching fire in the east wing, they would find a candle lit. Yet nobody ever went there. That windows and doors opened with nobody near them, that a night they heard this awful screaming and scratching. Dr Stroud put it down to rats. Daniel dwelled there alone now just Mary for company they became very close she posed for paintings. Daniels's ramblings got worse with time.

She did it, she will get me next, cannot you hear her calling screeching at me cannot you see her wandering about her manor waiting for a time to get me push me out of a window. I can hear her make it stop make it stop please Mary help me. I am not insane Mary you have to understand she did not leave that day. He had hold of Mary shaking her she was screaming Daniel please do not do this to me Daniel please I love you Daniel let go of me you are hurting me. He let go pleading it was a mistake he thought she was Eileen. Mary did not feel safe staying the night as Daniels's moods changed quickly. He said he saw John in the run-down stables with her. He claimed they were both after him. John to shut him up Eileen to kill him. His rambling became worse he told the Dr his head hurt all the time that he thought something was very wrong with him.

That night the Dr stayed with Daniel as he started to mumble she is here; she has come for me let me go Dr let me go. The Dr could not see anyone or hear anything. The Dr thought it best to commit him to the asylum his illness did not improve he became like a small child, he mumbled about her he wrote on the walls of his room with a pencil in very childish writing

At the stroke of midnight, she puts you to the test. She comes to you within your dreams will never let you rest. You the last in line she will haunt forever cursed the family Gaunt.

Just before he died, he scribbled on a piece of paper,

The mystery of Lysham Manor by NanyWytch

Seek the child Eileen Gaunt illegitimate. Child of my brother. He spent Years in the asylum, but he did not draw or paint or speak instead he simply sat there his mind gone. After his death he was interred in the family crypt on the grounds of the manor. The inscription was

Daniel Fredrick Gaunt died 13th November 1865

Lysham Manor stood proud and untouched apart from the valuation survey conducted by the lawyers of the estate.

The mystery of Lysham Manor by NanyWytch

Chapter 10 Examine.

This was to determine what amount of cash could be gained by selling it off to a buyer. For the purpose of a legacy. However, it was decided to leave it as it was after the surveyor returned as a gibbering wreck, talking about ghosts. Mary and Leah talked of it being a dark dismal place now the light had gone from it. The house seemed enveloped in a darkness all of its own making. Mary had served the family from a girl of 14 like Leah. They recalled how that placed used to thrive with all those staff. How it was full, of Elizabeth's laughter Fredrick chasing her as a young groom whilst they laughed together. The house was such a rich place in those days everyone wanted to work there. The Christmas ball was the best in the town, guests came from all over it had these huge trees all decorated, the servants were given brandy and port wine to have their own party below stairs whilst the other party was above stairs. She recalled being 14 years old coming from a really poor family, where they were lucky if they ate. Into this huge place where she ate 3 meals per day had a bed to herself, without fleas. That she had clean linen all the time, warm wool socks. The place had fires in all the rooms. The first time she saw the drawing room she was with Leah the same age they were to light the fire and tidy it up. Mary would touch things Leah would say do not we will get sacked. She recalled both boys running about the place, squealing or fighting over a toy. They had so much but did not ever seem satisfied. She recalled the mistress giving all the servants a Christmas gift and an orange. She had never been given a gift before it was a pair of boots for winter. She wanted to hug her, but it was considered unseemly. Boots new ones not already half worn out from the penny sale. These were black ankle boots with laces very nice, she had never tasted an orange before she savoured every last piece of it. It was the very first time anyone gave her a gift., Leah talked about her early days in the house too about how it was lively with dances. So much love and joy, if the walls had soaked up all that happiness how a little sadness could just change the manor so badly.

Francis Edward Baines n a respectable highly trained lawyer was given the case he had photos taken of the manor inside and out. He had all the furnishings covered in white cloth and listed with values next to them for the insurance company. He was to try trace an heir. All he was given was the scribbled note from a man in the asylum for 5 years. His job was all the harder as time drifted by many of those who had worked at the manor had either died or moved away the young Eileen had been sent away to Bingley Girls grammar school as a boarder aged 11, She was not known under the name Gaunt John had got a birth certificate printed with the name Eleanor n hunt his mother's maiden name. Sarah had remarried had another 8 children, so she too had moved when her two older sons had graduated Oxford University. They were a Dr, and a Lawyer ran their own practices in London.

As the years went the gates of the manor locked up long forgotten. The lawyer struggled in his quest eventually as with all legal cases it was shelved written on large legal papers in the back office.

Eleanor n grew into a lovely young lady; she was now 18 years old. Sarah had given her the name Hunt, the same as her other 11 children as John had paid for her and her two eldest go to private schools and universities, they were very well-educated Henry became a Dr, his brother Sam a lawyer& contriver by trade they made a good living. Eileen had not seen her mother Sarah in two years as she had been away Sarah died at aged 60 years.

Eileen was distraught at her death. So, any knowledge Sarah had was not passed to Eileen. She was a kindly girl always happy there was this glow of life within her so powerful it shone as bright as any lantern. Eileen had no knowledge of the manor House she had never seen it. The land was so overgrown you could not see the house at all. She loved Haworth Church the cobbled streets the cottages and the farming. Market day was one of her favourites she loved to make things, making her own clothing. All she knew of the manor was it was far behind these very high walls and a very rich family had once resided there. She had been told stay away from that place as its haunted.

1876 when a stranger called John Benson came to Haworth, he was a Contriver by trade. He was designing the new hospital, in Keighley to be called St John's the old one was crumbling needed redesigning which was being built where once there stood a thriving mill. But Haworth had quite a few mills this one had faded into the background. The villagers knew now of the billowing black soot coming from the 9 existing mills. The once small village had spread into a small town once the mills came. The main street had now green grocers two bakery, three butchers, the pharmacy. Lawyers &Drs offices, two taverns or now coaching houses. The haberdashery Eileen loved. Children ran along the streets playing but at 4am the streets were full of men women &

children walking to the mills. The sound of lots of wooden clogs on the cobbles echoed about, it was the same at 8pm when they came home.

Eileen had met John at a dance she attended, at New Year's Eve 1876 they became overly attached to each other she spent as much time as she could with this genuinely nice gentleman. It was obvious to all about that their acquaintance might lead to wedding bells. The following year they were married in 1879The wedding performed by Reverend William Annaud now an elderly man nearing retirement. The very same Reverend who had acted at the burials of most of the gaunt family.

Eleanor wore a beautiful chiffon gown of white, with a lace veil. She had lavender, roses and some broom in her posy. Eleanor looked so happy on the arm of her new husband, John was tall he was older than Eleanor she was just 29, he was 32 years old. The bells of the Chapel rang out with joy. They had a reception at the old tavern now called the coaching house in a private room. However, because john was the main designer for the hospital their honeymoon was put off. Instead, they had four days away in Yorkshire. Roaming the hills and countryside there. Had she only known of her real mother she might have found out more. Sarah had left her house to Eleanor has her sons had bought her a house in London which went to her other children. So, John and Eleanor lived here in the house she had grown up it. It held lots of very good memories for her. She had been a happy child.

The mystery of Lysham Manor by NanyWytch

Chapter 11. ghosts

Some weeks later John was walking past the huge iron gates of the manor wondering if this place might be worth investing monies into. From what he could see it looked wild and very unkempt. On enquiry he was told nobody had entered since the last occupant had died. He made more enquires purely based on his trade. His interest was value and design. He approached the lawyer in charge of the estate to enquire was it for sale? If it where it might be prevented from falling into further decay. No, he was told we are seeking the heir, if we do not find her soon it goes to the crown. This enhanced john's curiosity; the name of your heir Sir is? Francis Baines became interested in this gentleman they had dinner together, to talk about his interests in the old place he explained as a contriver by trade old buildings were something he admired. He said could I see the place just out of curiosity.?

Mr Baines thought well nobody else seems interested in the place maybe selling it would be a good move give the heir capital instead of a rundown estate. Almost in ruins now. His enquires had spanned 11 years now they had been fruitless he could not find a child of John gaunt registered anywhere. All he had were the writings of a lunatic. He had notes about a young lady arriving in Haworth but leaving just two years later now there was no trace of this woman meant to be the child's mother. Baines said it could not do any harm to go to the property, but he warned John it could be in a dangerous condition now. He gave him the set of keys asking they be returned as soon as he had finished his survey of the land and property. He asked if he might take some pictures of the manors condition if it were far too bad it might have to be pulled down. John set off to look at the old manor. The first thing to catch his eye was the emblazoned name designed into the gates some very fine blacksmithing indeed. Unlocking the gates, it took some energy just to push them open a small amount as brambles and ivy had grown on the otherwise. Bits of rust were now on his gloves. He brushed it away these were a gift from his wife he walked slowly had to clamber over a few fallen trees, he could see remnants of a very fine garden underneath the overgrown grasses, brambles and trees. As he neared the house, he shivered yet the sun was shining casting these rainbows through the trees, he could smell flowers yet could not see any. He felt it was a bit eerie. He considered 14 years decay but maybe it could be better than his first view looked like often sturdy old houses are designed to stand the test of time. He stood back surveying the sheer magnificent design of this place whosoever built this had a good eye. He tried to imagine the windows lit up with light. A happy atmosphere maybe a dance, but it quickly ebbed leaving him faced with unlocking this great oak door. The ivy had almost strangled al, the front of the house, wrapping about every crevice it could find he had to move some to just get to the door. It was engulfing the entire frontage trailing off around the pathways. Its tentacles were over the lintels of the door cutting into the stone. He had to force the key to turn with his pliers. But it then clicked loudly. Pushing with both arms he opened just one door, entering the hall he was hit with a thick wall, of cobwebs. Made him think of some huge spider hiding out of sight, but that was fantasy not truth. Dust like a thick carpet lay on the ground he moved some away with his foot to see the old roman tiles that would look so beautiful once cleaned up. Suddenly the door banged shut, yet no wind was about. He jumped at the sudden noise behind him. Its echoed rang through the house, so too did his footfalls sound through the entirety of the ground floor. They seemed to echoed back with a slight delay in time. John pulled his collar about his neck he felt suddenly very cold as if someone were breathing cold air onto him. He went upstairs first, wary of the floors testing each bit as he walked, he noticed silk rugs underfoot. Had everything simply be left there it did seem so. He walked around several bedrooms, then entered the room Eileen used to have with its curved window seat the window was open, he saw the picture of a very pretty young lady with a huge scratch over it as if someone had defaced this lovely painting on purpose. Something flew at him from a darkened corner it was a bird. He brushed it away from him opening the window for the bird. He felt a presence in the room, yet could see nothing, something brushed his neck. There was a smell of lavender and roses in the room, but the flowers were dead. He was impressed with the structural integrity of the place. He looked outside was shocked to see darkness coming in. It could not be that late surely not he had not even been here long. He walked around the drawing room; it was still furnished thing just had sheets over them. So, the heir gets a great place, structurally sound it simply needed some builders restore it. He saw the painting on the wall then he saw a painting that said John Gaunt, he stared at this picture that face those eyes those green bright eyes his wife had the same features. He read all the pictures Daniel Gaunt the artist there was another of that same woman that was so badly cut in the bedroom in this one the lady wore a ball gown of purple and a simple necklace a ribbon with a stone attached. She looked remarkably similar to his wife who is now 30, this woman may be around 20 no more. He just could not fathom in his head how this woman whom they said has not been here for a long time resembled his wife's features.

He decided to leave just as he entered the hall, he saw a woman walking down the stairs, hello he called out what are you doing here. But she walked right past him into the drawing room she did not make a sound he looked back into the room she was not to be found. He shivered stepping outside locking the door. He walked around the side of the house to where the stables once where it was a pile of old stones is all you could tell what it used to be as a stall still existed. He walked further to where the farm once was saw the ruined cottages over the other side thinking in its time this must have been a very beautiful place. He would really like to fix this up, but he would need see the plans. A drawing would be very useful too. He leaves the place locking up the gate as he turns to look back at the house, he sees a woman in a bedroom looking out at him. Maybe she was just in his mind as she had his wife's smile.

Strangest thing was inside the manors grounds dark clouds crawled the sky like monsters lurking in the darkness but once beyond the gate onto the road the sun shone the sky was blue it was warm with cotton wool clouds. He returns the keys to Mr Baines tells him about the pictures there especially the one looking like his wife. He invites him to dine with them asking if there was any paperwork about whom this woman was. Baines said just land documents and a will leaving it all to her. Yet she already owned a house in the village plus £20,000 oddly though that was now more like £60,000 as the money had been invested into oil. The account had around £10,000 in it. This had not been touched in 16 years. So, if the woman left,

The mystery of Lysham Manor by NanyWytch

she did so without her money. How very odd. Is the Reverend likely be at the Chapel at this time. Well, he may well be he has the family birth marriage and death dates in the Chapel books. He knew them all. Maybe he met the woman. Never asked said bane. I will ask for you, John why your interest in the place what is it like I have never been inside it creeps me out knowing how some of them died.

Dinner then at 8pm prompt, bring a friend with you please. He strolls off towards the church and sees the reverend sits talking to him for around an hour the reverend says he can produce copies of the certificate of birth marriages and death for all, of them. He was then asked had he met the woman in the painting in the drawing room, the Reverend said yes, she was so bright, and she smiled a lot. But she vanished without any trace the child and the Cook at the same time. Oh, I see, anyway we are having a dinner party tonight please do come it will be nice.

Thank you for your help I am thinking of buying the manor as an investment. Really is not there an heir, well there may well be but it sitting there decaying is not great. When I have the skills to rebuild it.

We will expect you for 8pm to dine please arrive around 7.30pm so we can look at your papers Mr bane is bringing what he has too. Oh, I see maybe fresh eyes will help solve the puzzle. Then see you tonight.

John walks back into the town to buy wines and brandy for the meal, he sees his wife tells her its six for dinner I invited some people over.

The mystery of Lysham Manor by NanyWytch

OK we are having lamb tonight I will add more veg, so we have enough my love and desert what you would like, oh now they look nice get 6 of those. They were in the bakers, she bought 6 large custards and two loaves of bread plus a chocolate and strawberry cake. We will be fat after this love. Truly yes, we will.

That night when over dinner the men talked about the Gaunt family home Lytham manor Eileen got a cold shiver run down her back. Reverend Annaud told them about the family and said that place was the most productive farmland in the area when Frederick and Elizabeth were alive but after he died the place went rack and ruin within two years now it has been emptied for 14 years. They have no idea what happened to the woman Frederick spoke of in his will. Her property had not been touched he said a neighbour had the keys to the cottage that they might go see it. Find out if any paperwork existed about her. John said he could go Eleanor wanted go too. It seems it was only down the next street. They all retired as the two men stayed overnight in the guest rooms.

Next day after a long breakfast they go to the house, it was a quiet big place inside nothing had been covered over. Dust was extremely thick like a carpet had been laid over the floors. cobwebs stretched everywhere. But there was a chest in the bedroom John looked inside whilst the Reverend and Eleanor searched the study the only papers were years old. The only letter they saw was from Eileen Mason Perry to her aunt jess saying she was on her way to see her. They decided this must be the woman whom Sir Fredrick left his manorial lands and manor too. It was spelt the same and the dates fit. They found birth certificate of Eileen Mason Perry she would have been only 19 years old the same age as she was right now. She wished there were pictures, but none were found. They went out to lunch Mr Blaine said he would do more digging based on this birth date. He said deaths are registered with the same number as birth so they could find her. Or it might lead them to the heir.

That night John slept badly; he was dreaming about the face he saw in that painting in the drawing room. John recalled how dark and cold it was. That creepy feeling of someone touching his neck. His dream took him back into the manor but in it he was walking past the stairs towards the back stairs he rounded a corner right at the top of these stairs was a door it opened on its own. It went to a stone staircase; he walks down here to the wine cellar one of the tall shelves began to move. It slid on this arc marked on the floor like a secret door. Behind it was a wall, that looked newer than the others he touched it with his hand and these letters appeared in plaster

October 12, 1858 I who lie uneasy here will, haunt forever year on year till this place in ruins lie only then will evil die.

He turned to push the shelf back but then saw a girl the exact image of his wife. He woke suddenly seeing Eleanor standing at the window in their own cottage. She said John I had a terrible dream. Please hold me. He held his wife saying nothing of his own nightmare. John was puzzled about the room behind the shelf, he wanted see the plans of the manor, but he could not find another room behind a tall shelf. When he arrived home his wife was sitting near the fire reading these legal papers sent round by messenger addressed to Mrs

The mystery of Lysham Manor by NanyWytch

Benson. John sat with her reading the papers it seemed research showed that Eileen Mason Perry had registered a female child born 30 years ago. It did not mention a father, so it was marked illegitimate under law normally children born this way were not normally given inheritance unless no direct blood relatives were living that were legitimate. Eleanor said so it is mine John all of it. Yes, my love it is. What would you like to do? I think we need think long term. When you saw it does it need more than cleaning right now. Yes, love we need builders to repair it rebuild some areas. But we ought to start with the manor, the garden will, need a few workers for months. The house needs to be cleaned plus your new status means you will need employ staff as you cannot care for a place like that alone. John said hugging his wife, maybe we should sell it off. I felt something very creepy when inside there. John, it has been empty is all once it cleaned up it will be great for us. John, we cannot just sign it away I have not even seen it. First, we ought to go see it decide what we need to do make it nice. So darling now your wife is very rich what do you feel about her. You can now open your own offices begin designing more than the hospital my love. You can redesign the manor.

The mystery of Lysham Manor by NanyWytch

Chapter 11 haunted

Here Dr Stroud ended his story of lysham manor. John had sat paying absolute attention so as far as we know its fact. Yet we have no actual proof how much. I am old now so am handing the business of my patients to Paul my son I want spend my retirement in my garden. I failed to help Daniel so it worries me that I might fail your lovely lady too. Maybe we both need a stiff drink brandy he offers yes please makes a change from tea. Tea remarks John yes, it is what is normally offered to Drs

Eleanor became more distant with each day at the manor, she refused to employ a companion instead she asked her best friend one of Sarah's girls move in with them giving her the corner room with the curved window seat. The picture near the window was dispensed with far too damaged to repair.

John decided he would look around the parts of the house he had not seen yet. He took a lamp exploring the east wing. This had been closed off when Daniel was alive. The builders were fixing up the west wing and had started on the North wing. John took a lamp and began exploring he had his structural engineer with him.

He encountered what could have been the master's bedroom it contained a four-poster bed. Actually still, made up but covered with a dirty white cloth. A dresser stood near the window with a big family bible on it. A large painting of a gentleman dominated the room. He viewed around ten rooms all still furnished. Some plaster needed replacing a few floorboards and a few doors. But mostly it was sound. Some windows needed replacing. His engineer said shall we check out the attic rooms or what would have been servants' quarters. They moved some heavy velvet curtains dust made them cough. Climbing up the back stairs to the next floor. It contained 10 small rooms some with nothing in them, some with metal bed frames and small set of draws. One room had a painting of a child of around a few months in the same room were a lot of very dark paintings one such painting had red background and this skeletal creature with twisted nails and Spindly fingers its face like a person screaming the mouth wide open but the eyes were darkened pools it was very frightening yet there were more three creates full they mostly had these spindly fingers in them.

In a box here he found a large metal key. Plus, one smaller key maybe to the desk in the drawing room. Back down on first floor they entered a room that obviously belonged to a woman. Hung in the wardrobe were dresses so lovely he thought his wife would look very sophisticated wearing one especially the purple one with embroidered collar. A hairbrush and comb lay on the dresser. A wall sign embroidered read god bless this house. Another painting hung here near the window a most beautiful woman the label said Elizabeth Gaunt. Another painting hung in the corridor of another woman on horseback who looked like his wife. It read Eileen Mason Perry 1875

During this time as John and the engineer went down to the kitchens it was now all clean there was a laundry room pantry storeroom the coal cellar and the boot room still, having pairs of riding boots in here 6 pairs plus waterproof coats hats. There were the cooks sitting room the servants dining room it was all laid out as it was when the place had over 26 staff. John read a ledger that must have been the cooks. It had menus, then lists of goods bought with costs each page was one week. It appeared she had a housekeeping budget for food.

But the wine ledger was interesting they bought 100 bottles of fine champagne for a party. 200 bottles of mixed wine, 50 bottles fine French brandy 30 of whiskey and 60 of port wine. It would mean the wine cellar would be extremely full refilled every 3 months.

The engineer said they knew how to live these people, wonder if those boots fit me. John said try them do you ride? Yes, well if they fit keep them. his engineer George found two pairs that fit him size 11s, so he was told they were his. The room they opened with the large key was the gun room. It was full of shotguns all, different types some were so beautiful John said I am liking this very much imagine just saying today we can have a shoot keep down the ducks and pheasants. But missing were the shells he did not find one box. He was disappointed.

During this time, the engineer and John were recording all repairs. So, they could get things done. The North Wing was mainly unstable John decided that this could be demolished. The stone used for rebuilding the stables. Or the farm cottages they could give to staff working on the land clearing fields. That way the whole family could stay together.

Meanwhile Eleanor was with her friend in the drawing room moving things about. She took pictures off the walls as she wanted the painting of them behind the dresser. She wanted these paintings moved to the hall. She enjoyed having another woman about the place they changed the whole layout of the drawing room, to suit their lives now they retained the card table. She did the girly nesting thing making rooms have a feminine touch. Adding clothes and flowers plants, her mother's pottery the very nice blue and green Daulton set. She had employed a cook, a downstairs maid, upstairs maid two of them. A valet and a butler plus 3 gardeners, they employed 20 farm labourers to clear the land the place was a hive of activity. Decorators inside as she wanted walls painted, they had the ivy trimmed back. The gates and driveway cleaned. For the first three months they were never alone at the manor. John and his team worked quickly they brought in anyone they needed. Eleanor could not get used to being called miss or ma'am John was addressed as Sir by his workers, so it did not bother him. Eleanor liked to go sit with the cook giving her recipes. They worked out menus for three months. Everything was going very smoothly until Eileen started having nightmares.

John had gone down to the kitchens then walked outside into the courtyard, he walked to the newly built stables seeing two horses tethered there he saw a young man there he said to him do you live around here? I come from the farm over the hill Sir; these yours then lad? No Sir I saw them here, so fed them and was petting them. Yes, they are lovely. I suppose you do not know who owns them, no Sir not me. My pa was a stable boy here at my age if you be needing one, I do not mind Sir. But I would live at home just come over each day. My pa told me about the back way into here. What back way. Come with me I will show you servants came in this way. He showed John another gate hidden in the bushes. It led out onto main street. John offered the boy half a crown tells him what he knew about the place. The lad said I am not ever held this much money Sir, but nobody really knew the family they did not mix with lesser you see. Master Daniel was the only one who really spoke to people kindly he owned the art gallery Sir, does this mean you own it now. Suppose that a yes. I wonder if I might speak with your father could you ask him when it is a good time call up. Thou should come now at 4pm its milking so between 2pm and 3pm he takes a break will be sitting in the kitchen with my mother. John walked over with this lad called Edward. Marshall Roche was this farmer. He told John about what he knew of the family saying once the lady came the master Fredrick really cheered up. But when John and Daniel came home for new year's, the master was very upset for the first time he sold four acres off pay off johns gambling debts. After he died everything changed and a few months after this more land got sold off. My farm used to be part of the estate. I bought it from Daniel after John fell out the window caving his head in. Daniel did not come out the lady just vanished with the Cook and the baby sir. The lawyer closed the place up and it stayed that way. Thank you,

I saw a woman in the window you say john fell from no Sir that cannot be by time he fell only staff were two maids and a cook. Eileen had been long gone. Staff left because of strange things happening in the east wing when nobody used it. What do you mean well Daniel said odd things Sir like she was here she never left? what if she was here what if she never left like he said But Daniel was rabbling so it is possible he was imagining the whole thing I doubt it Sir strange things happen here especially in that wing we no longer use?

The mystery of Lysham Manor by NanyWytch

So, you think my wife's mother is here somewhere well Sir you said none of her money has ever been used. Which to me says she was dead afore John and Daniel Sir, thanks it may answer some questions I have for the Dr. Glad to help Sir if you need a hand over their eddy is a good lad, he works for me mornings but afternoons he could work for you he wants learn engineering. My other sons will get the farm my twins. If he worked with you, he might have some great ideas. Back at the manor the kitchen staff had found a blocked off door. John fumbles in his pocket finds the oldest key it fit he turns it yes, a click that says open. He and his engineer went down with lanterns the missing wine cellar. Walking down these steps they were sloppy, so damp was in here. The stench of the mould here was terrible. The floor had an inch of stagnant water on it. But where was it from? Old bottles of wine covered in cobwebs graced a few shelves a cask of brandy lay on its side. Along with a case of whiskey from Scotland. They took two bottles out for upstairs

He felt like he had seen this place before, the engineer said maybe an underground stream exists under the foundations we will need dig it out find out and to fix it up the following week they began breaking up the floor find the leak it took a lot of hard work with several men to fix it relay a new floor. Indeed, but have you seen how thick this wall is. He saw this curved scratch on the floor, so he looked for a lever. Finding it the shelf slid opening up another small room, an axe lay on the floor. He saw scratches appear on the wall, he turned said Jack look! Oh my god where did that come from? John said in his dream he was in this room but when he turned girl was there but where is she? What is she? Whom is she?

The mystery of Lysham Manor by NanyWytch

Up in the library John found the small, key fit the old desk inside was a book. In it was a list of names

Sir Fredrick John Gaunt received the hand in marriage of miss Elizabeth angelicas 1835

John gaunt born 9th March 1836 died 1855

Daniel gaunt 8pm 11th February 1839 died 1865

Lady Elizabeth died 1845 during childbirth the baby named jade gaunt. died with her mother. Aged 35

Fredrick John Gaunt died July 13th, 1858 aged 55.

This brought him no closer to his goal of finding his wife's mother. Eleanor became worse she would scream holding her hands over her ears in the night, she began not sleeping again saying she could see a woman who looked like her in the mirrors. She covered up all the mirrors in the house or she smashed them. Odd thing was John would find her in that east room with the curved window sitting in the window singing a song he had not heard before. When he asked her oh that my mother sang it? Your mother Sarah no silly my mother. Ok he said come down to the drawing room rose is worried about you. No need I am fine really, I am. John I think I should leave here soon can we go away now most of the works done. Of course, my love where was you thinking? Can we go to Cornwall? Anywhere you wish. A trip was planned for a couple of weeks away, whilst they were away Eleanor went back to being her bubbly self no nightmares no screaming fits no vanishing for hours. She looked a picture of health. John was puzzled by the vast changes in his wife. It was like the manor ate her energy but when away she was well again. He wanted check it out now they had lived at the manor 15 months. Coming back from the holiday they held a party for Eleanor's birthday. She danced really enjoyed herself now she was 30 years old. Eleanor danced and sang she enjoyed the night, all the guests stayed over in various rooms. During the night some came from their rooms saying they heard scratching, and someone had let a bird into the upstairs it flew around in a mad panic then flew into the window with a crash. John picked it up it was still alive but badly hurt so he snapped its neck then took it outside. He tried to work out how the bird got into the upstairs parts of the house.

Within a month of being back in the manor the terrors returned, John was so upset at this deterioration again in his wife he talked with Dr Paul Stroud who told him Daniel talked about a woman in mirrors and the painting he did in the asylum when first there were really dark, but all featured some woman. If something had happened to her mother inside this house then maybe your wife is being haunted and simply is not sick as we might think. If this person body lies here somewhere on finding it the haunting should cease maybe we could talk to the spiritualist movement. I heard they can talk to spirits.

John burst out laughing you are not serious tell me you are pulling my leg you're actually seriously thinking this is how to proceed. Paul, I do not want do anything that will make my wife worse. Sleeping drafts help but we cannot simply keep her asleep. Eleanor's tortured state is constantly on john's mind now. He feels helpless, Dr Stroud arrives for his evening visit he says leaving her is the worst we can do if she is sleeping soundly calmly her body and mind are at rest. John worries that in this drugged state she could be living in the nightmare unable to wake. John did some digging into Daniels's life he visited the asylum with the Dr, it was a huge ghastly place. Daniel being a gentleman Had his own room, most just shared a big room. Inside this room was one mattress on a wooden bed frame nothing else. But the walls, floor and evening the ceiling had been painted in these terrible drawings of this creature with twisted long skeletal finger and claws, a dark face with black holes as eyes, and worst of all its mouth was wide open. It might have once been a woman, but you could not tell because of all the red paint smeared everywhere. There were bits of paper with scribbling on them. The Dr got to see the medical file it said he had been admitted with severe instability caused by delusions something was trying to kill him. He suffered night terrors, did not sleep much, the diagnosis was severe delusional state. Which could mean anything the Dr said treatment had been recorded as baths and swirling chairs which were terrible. He was kept well sedated due to his violent outbursts at the staff claiming it was in his room he needed get out. In a wooden box there were some good pictures one of an old man called Symons, one of his brother John at harvest time, one of both his parents, and finally one of a women on horseback whom had to be his wife's mother as the likeness was unmistaken.

The mystery of Lysham Manor by NanyWytch

Chapter 12 Enlightenment

During the night Eleanor wakes feeling much better, she had one thing on her mind find and destroy what it trying drive her insane.

Slipping out the bed in her long white nightgown, she walks downstairs in the dark. Goes to the drawing room the fire in there still warm, she sits still on the fender. Suddenly putting her hands to her head hearing the voices again. Help me help me please get me out help me. It echoes inside her head. Then she sees the woman, her face distorted her skeletal fingers with long twisted nails, her hair down past her thighs all draping over her. Help me Eleanor helps me. It leads her to the kitchens, then to the cellar, she picks up a lantern from near the old door. It is hard to push open, she almost falls down these stone steps. Holding onto the wall as she edges down, her feet slide on this green dampness she takes it very slowly following the ghostly apparition. Wondering why it was now showing her things.

Suddenly the door slammed shut loudly behind her, Eleanor panicked ran back up the slippery steps. Opens the door holding up the lantern she looks down. The woman seems to vanish behind a shelf. She then sees her on the stairs right in front of her, drops the lantern that rolls down the stairs the glass breaks igniting the straw from the packing cases. The smoke turns thick black because of the damp. She struggled open the door which was trying close itself. This ghostly woman was holding it shut laughing the smoke is choking her she is banging on the door, shouting John help me help me. The apparition is smiling at her whilst holding the door closed.

The mystery of Lysham Manor by NanyWytch

It touches her face pretty little girl mummy would not want you a product of rape. The smoke grew even thicker she slumps on the stairs rolls down them, passes out the flames are growing only a few more boxes but the whiskey, wine and brandy starts to spread its wetness over the floor spraying glass everywhere as the alcohol burns. John woke suddenly seeing his wife missing, knowing her state of mind he walks downstairs. He looks in rooms, then in the kitchen, he sees the glow from the cellar, flames come out at him like a hungry monster wanting air. He shuts the door stop it spreading then he throws buckets and buckets of water down. Once it is out, he walks in. His wife is badly burnt on her feet legs arms he lifts her limp lifeless body carries her upstairs to the sofa in drawing room. wakes up the valet send him on horseback fetch the Dr quickly.

The air was cold everywhere silent and still, dawn was starting to break the sun cast its first light a cross the darkness of the sky.,. They go back in the Drs trap. Once inside Dr says it will more than likely be asphyxiation smoke on the lungs. But doing a post-mortem will tell, them all they need to know. He looks at the burns to her feet hands. They are not that deep it is like the flames licked her but did not really set her alight. After 3 weeks they are told death by misadventure. John cannot deal with his young wife's death after the quiet funeral he leaves cornfield for a month to work on some building in London.

When he returns, he is a changed man he is thinking about his wife's description of her tormentors. He then goes to the asylum asking to read Daniels's file. He reads the very same descriptions in his own words. So, he takes up Dr Stroud on the spiritualists coming to the house.

The night is dark a storm rages across the sky, 6 people arrive they say they are from the movement. They claim to be able contact his wife or any disembodied spirits in the manor. Setting up around the table. They light candles burn incense and have a Ouija board to talk to the dead, John does not really believe in it but is going along with it see if anything actually does work. The medium says no matter what happens they must not let go of hands during this as its very important not to break our circle swear to me you will all abide by these rules. It will protect us. They all agree to this condition.

They start whilst holding Eleanor's necklace, the room goes darker the candles start to waver about, then the banging starts. The medium says there are many spirits here on stronger than the others. Then the candles all blow out as a wind crosses the table. One of them lights them again, the medium says do not let go of hands it is very important do not break our circle. Banging comes again then right on the table in soot is the words, at the stroke of midnight she will put you to the test, for you the last in line will haunt forever cursed the family Gaunt the words were signed Danny. The medium said Daniel speaks to us tell us what happened here. A big wind blew out the candles Daniels painting fell to the floor with a big crash, on the back of the picture was a small key. The word desks. Nothing more candles re lit, another presence is here she says its dark selfish angry. She says John Gaunt, are you with us the table rocks a bit. Tell us about the girl. A dismembered voice speaks through the medium, she is dead is it not enough. Set me free set me free she holds onto me. Give me freedom from her.

Then the medium collapses, a few minutes pass, she raises her head a really lovely girls voice is there. Find me help me find me help me. The medium says that is all for one session.

We can do another day after tomorrow; I can bring others the thing is extraordinarily strong. They leave Dr Stroud says so what was your thoughts here. Not sure but I have seen those words at the asylum, Daniel did write them. Do you think the other voice was his brother, I doubt it maybe someone pretended be him?

Nobody knows what he did or what he was like now only one painting had John in it. With his mother as a toddler.

John went down to the cellar with the Dr saying why was she here, the place is huge. Why here? They look around then John says to the Dr its staring us in the face, my dreams, Eileen's dreams the words. He pulls the shelf open along the curve on the floor. Look at the other walls. This is not the same. In a dream I was in here words were on the wall written in blood. Get the axe. The Dr hits the plaster with the axe it crumbles down in chunks with lots of dust. John gets another axe from the tools down there. They keep hitting the wall, gradually a hole appears, and a few stones are moved. Then they see the skull with its mouth wide open its fingers with long nails curved over. The hair almost covering the body They pull more away. The body is folded up. The Dr fetch a white sheet he lays it out on the ground. Its female he says this is more than likely Eileen your wife's mother. She might have been here over 16

The mystery of Lysham Manor by NanyWytch

years Just then the door slams shut a screeching howling comes banging on the walls is happening its noise wakes the staff who run outside. John and the Dr run outside too as all the windows and doors start to open and shut banging. John says this is enough takes a candle lights it once the staff are all outside, he sets fire to the curtains in the drawing room and library. Comes outside watches the manor burn to the ground. he said to the Dr we were all blind it was in the writings.

The manor now burnt-out ruins, John stands amongst them, tears running down his face. Dr Stroud says it has over now come stay with me. The curse broken he sees his wife walking towards him through the debris. She touches his face, smiles at him whispering we are all free my love thanks you they witness several spirits leaving They simply fade away he smiles watching his wife and others leave Lysham Manor Dr Stroud takes his arm come now stay with me it has done it is over now I must think of you my dear friend They walk away together locking the wrought iron gates turning one last time to see the manor in all its glory of bygone days it looked as if it had rebuilt itself.

Word count 38 ,166 words

The mystery of Lysham Manor by NanyWytch